A NOVEL OF YOUNG LOVE

The PALE BLONDE
of
SANDS STREET

WILLIAM CHAPMAN WHITE

ABRIDGED EDITION

POPULAR LIBRARY • NEW YORK

POPULAR LIBRARY EDITION

*COMPLETE AND
UNABRIDGED*

Published by arrangement with The Viking Press, New York

1.

*M*ANY NAVY MEN KNOW SOME OF this story but it's unlikely they'll be telling it. Too many questions would follow about what they were doing at the time.

The captain of the battleship *Kansas* saw her one evening when he was alone in his quarters ruffling a card deck for a late game of solitaire. The chief engineer on the cruiser *Syracuse* saw her late at night as he was ordering full speed ahead to make land by daybreak. Two seamen on the destroyer *Manasquan* saw her but they weren't surprised because it's well known that that old tub is haunted. An ensign on the destroyer *Milton* saw her on deck one evening as he was hurrying to the bridge with a handful of papers. They went flying. He had a bad hour explaining how he happened to let go of those papers in a high wind. He couldn't make anyone believe he'd seen a blonde on board who asked him one question, waited a second for an answer, then disappeared.

The boatswain's mate on the minelayer *Licon* saw her in the forward hold. He was about to throw her in irons, but when he tried it he got the shock of his life. Schwartz, machinist's mate third class on the *Ountelaunee*, saw her and told his shipmates about her in an excited whisper. He was always bragging about women and nobody believed him, even though he searched the ship for the next three days. The landing officer on the carrier *Crown Point* swore he saw her on the flight deck at night just as a Hornet was landing. He lost sight of her for a second, after screaming something and waving his paddles. The plane landed. When the officer looked again the girl was still there, her pale hair blowing in the wind. Then he really screamed.

It was the same on the *Wyomissing,* the *Tuscaloosa,* the *Grunton,* the *Biloxi,* the *Asquantee,* the *Pensacola,* the *Albuquerque,* and many other ships. Some man on each one of them saw her. Most of them could describe her but their descriptions varied. Few of them ever called her beautiful. Most of them could tell how her hair was the color of the pale gold sunset on those rare Pacific evenings when the sun settles quietly, modestly, not throwing great flamboyant cloudbursts of color, but staying round and golden and settling on a sheet of molten green and yellow gold just above the deep blue sea. They could tell you about her eyes too, not their color, but about the living flame in them, like the heat and light seen through the little peering window of the flaming boilers of a pounding ship.

But they won't tell you because it's small pleasure to be laughed at for such a story.

*   *   *

Sands Street runs through lower Brooklyn like a varicose vein. It leads from the main gate of the Navy Yard to the subway stations. It is a tough, knotted street of saloons, laundries, tattoo parlors, dry cleaners, groceries, Coffee Pots, and lodgings. Its stores sell clothes, trinkets, watches, photographs, and anything else to snatch at a sailor's dollar. Every service is marked "While you wait." Trolleys grind along its narrow width. Shabby curtains flap from its upstairs windows where the shadeless glare of light bulbs marks cheap shelter for the night. From the cellars of the old buildings comes a clammy sour odor as if brackish salt water were seeping under them.

It is the first touch of America for many sailors when they hurry out on shore after months at sea. As they rush for the subway and Manhattan, it is a long street. For others who walk it back to the Yard, hand in hand with a girl for the last time, it is the shortest street in the world.

Most of the time the street has as little beauty as the

neon signs that light its shop windows, or the mangy cats that slip in and out of the cellars, forever lured by their fishy smell. But on some summer mornings the soft mist slips in from the harbor and folds the street in gray silver. Then it is a place fit for miracles and strange high wonders.

On such a morning, so early that the stars were still over her, Katie came along the street, walking as light as breath. In gray jacket and skirt she was part of the mist, blown for the moment into something tall and lovely.

Out of the fog came a sailor, hurrying as they all do when leaving the Yard. He was built slim and tall, hipless as a young poplar, with the swing of a rising deck in his step. In the tilt of his hat, in the way he walked, were promise of impudence and the simple ageless strength of youth.

As he passed Katie he said pleasantly, "Hiya!"

"Hello, sailor!" Katie's voice was low and throaty.

"Well!" He sounded surprised that anyone should answer. "Where you going?"

"To work," Katie said, with no hint of any particular hurry.

"At this time of the morning?"

"I work in a restaurant. People have to eat early."

"What's your name?"

"Katie Morrison. What's yours?"

"Johnny, Johnny Smith." He stood with his hands on his hips, swinging on his heels, not sure what to do next or what he wanted to do next. Then he laughed softly. "Anyway, it's a miracle."

Katie liked the warmth of his voice, the laughter in his words. "What's a miracle?"

"We just docked and I got only twelve hours' liberty. The first thing I wanted to do on shore was to talk to a girl," he continued, his smile broadening. "Baby, you don't know what that means to a sailor." He shifted from one foot to the other. "And here I am, talking to a girl."

"You make it sound like a prayer."

Johnny rubbed his hands on the sleeves of his jumper. "I'm cold. Come on and have a drink."

"I have to be at the restaurant at six."

"You have time for a cup of coffee," Johnny said in the manner of a man accustomed to taking over. "Maybe breakfast too. I never met a woman yet who turned down breakfast when I asked her."

Katie hesitated for only a moment. In the poor light Johnny's face was not clear but his voice was boyishly warm and friendly. She said, "It's a funny time to be taking a girl to breakfast."

Johnny shook that one aside. "Sailors are always doing funny things." And he took her arm with great sureness.

And that's how the story starts, and little fresh or new about it. Sailor meets a girl, talks with her, and off they go together. And that happens numberless times in Brooklyn, Antwerp, Manila, or Valparaiso, whether it be foggy, clear, starlit or starless.

Arm in arm they went along, their footsteps loud in the deserted street. The first clear morning light showed in the east, wan and washed of color. At the sound of their steps a dog came bellyscraping from a doorway. "Here, Rover, Tippy!" Johnny called. To Katie he said, "You never see girls on shipboard and you miss them, but you miss dogs too, because you never see them either." The dog came closer, his tail wagging. Johnny stooped to him and the dog scooted away. "Hm," Johnny grunted, "he doesn't think much of sailors!"

At the corner ahead was an all-night coffee shop, gray-white, like a maid's dirty uniform. Johnny pointed to it. "That looks pretty swell."

"It's only a Coffee Pot."

"Anything that doesn't have a chowline waiting ahead of me looks swell. Let's go in."

The lone attendant was reading a newspaper, making notes at the same time on a scratch pad. He looked annoyed at any interruption. Johnny greeted him but got no answer.

"You don't seem awful glad to see us," Johnny said.

"Customers ain't no treat these days." Unwillingly, pencil and paper went down.

Johnny looked to Katie for some explanation. She said, "He wouldn't last long in Lushman's Restaurant, Branch Eighty-two, where I work."

"Bring us coffee, eggs and bacon," Johnny ordered.

"Too early for eggs. Haven't come yet."

"Double order of bacon."

"Too late for bacon. All gone."

Johnny grinned at Katie. "We better fill up on coffee and buns."

"Anything, Johnny." It had been a long time since she had breakfasted anywhere except behind the counter at Lushman's.

Johnny pushed back his hat until it seemed to hang on his head by a hair. He lit a cigarette and smiled. "This is pretty nice. Who'd have imagined it, six hours ago, when we were coming down the Sound? I could tell from your voice out there on the street that you were pretty. You got nice eyes and hair too. I never saw hair that color."

Katie said, "I'm Irish."

"I was in Ireland and never saw anyone like you," Johnny answered. "Lots of guys must have told you you're pretty."

"If you say it, no one else ever needs to," Katie assured him. She was eager to store away deep in her mind the imprint of his face. It was young, almost unbearded. Its strength shone in it. His eyes were gray and almost too soft for the stolidity of jaw and for the firmness of his forehead. His mouth was soft, and its smile could light his face. Without that smile he looked hard and mature. Smiling, he looked like such a little boy.

Katie said, "You don't seem old."

"I'm twenty-four."

"That's not so old."

Johnny looked slightly disgusted and pushed his hat back. The hat had a hard time staying on a heavy wave of dark hair. He said, "In the Navy, baby, you age fast. I bet I've seen as much as guys in civvies see before they're sixty. I bet I know more about all kinds of things, different sorts of things, than guys who work in stores or factories or even in the Army."

The attendant brought the coffee and buns and thumped them down. "Hey, Mac, you interested in horses?"

"Huh?" Johnny looked up surprised. "Say, how many horses do you think I see in the Navy?"

"You don't see many women either, but what else do you talk about?" the counterman pointed out. "Take my advice, Mac, horses are better than women. You always know horses'll let you down and then you ain't so surprised when they do. Now and then sometimes they don't and you get a pleasant surprise. But you never expect women to let you down and then they do and how do you feel? And that's why women are worse than horses."

Katie snorted. "And what about men?"

"Men! Say, do you really want me to tell you about men?"

"No, thanks," Katie snapped. The counterman retreated, rebuffed.

Katie's glance followed him. "These restaurant guys are all alike. Horses and women, that's all they know. And whether it's horses or women, they're always looking for what they call sleepers." She thought of Joe, counterman at Lushman's Eighty-two. He'd have the coffee urns going by now and he'd be pretty sore at her for being late.

The attendant called from the counter, "I know a lot more than horses and women, sister."

Katie asked sharply, "Would you be feeling put upon if I said mind your own business and figure out your day's bets?"

"I got a better way to make dough on horses than bet on them," he answered, taking up paper and pencil.

Johnny glanced at her with admiration. "You certainly know how to talk to him. And if you want to know anything about men, ask me."

Katie grinned at him.

"Women too," Johnny said. "Boy, we sailors know our

women." He drank his coffee quickly and put down the cup. "We ought to. We think enough about them."

"I like sailors," Katie answered.

"I could tell that." Johnny was pleased. "There's two kinds of women in the world, those who know how to handle sailors and those who don't." He spoke with great sureness. "I was down in Trinidad once. They got beautiful girls there—Spanish, Chinese, Negro, and Hindoo, all mixed together. There was one little one I knew, mostly Chinese. I took her away from a soldier after a hell of a fight. I got so banged up she took me to her place to fix me up and damn if everything in her house hadn't come off American ships—things sailors brought to her. I just had a hunch when I saw her she was a sailor's girl."

Katie looked at him closely, trying hard to make that story fit a face like his, but because he was pleased with himself she smiled. "The trouble with sailors," Katie said with authority, "is that you go with them to the Sands Street gate and then you never see them again."

"That's the way sailors are," Johnny agreed. He called to the attendant, "More coffee." Then he noticed the clock on the wall. "Only five-thirty and I got a whole day's liberty. Well, maybe not a whole day, but twelve hours anyway."

"You have to go back so soon?"

"Five p.m."

For ten minutes Katie had been barely holding back the thought that she would have to leave him shortly. She had hoped that perhaps this evening they could meet, but this day would have no evening. Then she heard herself say, "It's time I was going. Joe'll be awful sore if I'm late."

Johnny's smile vanished. "You can stay for one more cup of coffee."

Katie hesitated for a moment, then agreed. For so many mornings she had walked to work through gray and red dawn and imagined a man coming along and him saying, "Miss Morrison, Miss Katie Morrison, the captain presents his compliments and would you be breakfasting on his yacht at five-thirty a.m. sharp?" That never happened but if it had, Lushman's Eighty-two would have had to operate without one of its countergirls for that day. Coffee now with Johnny was better than any breakfast any captain or any yacht anywhere could provide.

She frowned at the clock. "I have to go soon."

Johnny agreed, "I guess you do."

Once again the counterman brought coffee. "Excuse me for interrupting but your crack about my betting on horses stuck in my crop."

"What do you do with horses?" Katie asked. "Sing to them?"

"Every time a horse wins a race, it stands to show, doesn't it, that it must have been for a reason," he answered with pitying condescension. "If you could find that reason and work it out you'd have a secret worth a lot of money, wouldn't you, huh?"

Katie snorted. "These guys have to stand on their feet so much they start dreaming every time their corns ache."

The counterman ignored that. "That's what I do, try to find the reason. It could be any one of a lot of things or maybe a combination—the weight, the condition of the track, the initial the jockey's name begins with, the number of letters in the trainer's name"—he went on without a breath—"any one of fifty or sixty things. Even the influence of the moon, maybe, or the temperature. It stands to reason, doesn't it?"

"Maybe the horse's feelings have something to do with it," Katie said, "and how do you find those out?"

"I been working for six months on a formula," the counterman continued confidentially. "If you can find a formula in anything, boy, you got a way to make a living. That's all you need to get on in this world, a formula, but boy, you gotta have it. Now, you take horses—"

"Take 'em right back to the counter with you," Katie said, "and tie 'em up tight. That's all I hear on my job all day."

The attendant shook his head. "That's what's wrong with the world, nobody wants to listen. Everybody wants to talk." He returned to his counter, his head still shaking. "Nobody wants to listen."

"I don't know what he's talking about," Johnny said. He pushed his hat back, then let his chair rear on its hind legs. He smiled at Katie. "Boy, this is nice. After five months at sea it's even nice to sit with a girl in a dump like this. That's what you do in the Navy, dream about what you're going to do when you're on shore again."

"What do you dream about?"

"This time I came ashore to do five things."

"What are they?"

"Oh, various sorts of things," Johnny said, pleased at possessing a bit of mystery. "Meeting a girl was the first but I didn't expect to do it so soon. They're hard to find at five in the morning."

"I guess so."

"A shipmate of mine, Lardlips—"

"What's his name?"

"A foreign name, something like Lardlips, so that's what we call him. He said you couldn't find a girl in New York before noon. That's probably when the kind of dames he knows gets up." Johnny glanced out of the window. A few people were on the sidewalks. Sands Street was coming slowly alive. "I wish Lardlips would come by right now."

Katie nodded. She had the tones of his voice memorized, the deep tone that preceded laughter, the firm note of pride, the lightness of his amusement, the boyish eagerness when he explained something.

"There's another thing I dreamed about on shipboard, but you'll think it's funny," Johnny confessed.

"No, I won't," Katie said, watching the way a smile formed on his face.

"It's awful kid stuff."

"I'll bet it isn't."

"Grass."

"Grass?"

"That's what I dream about sometimes," Johnny said, lowering his voice. "You don't see any grass on shipboard but where I was raised on a farm it was all around like water."

"I never was on a farm," Katie admitted.

"I never want to be on another one," Johnny answered with sudden bitterness. "I used to hate having nothing but fields and grass, but not having them made me think about them, I guess."

Katie nodded. "That's just like Lushman's Eighty-two. I took three days off once because I was fed up, but I spent most of the time wondering about what was going on there."

"I know," Johnny nodded, finishing his coffee.

Katie looked once again at the clock. "I'm awful sorry but I have to go."

Johnny promptly left his side of the white-topped table and sat beside her.

He looked sharply at her. "I never saw a girl with eyes like yours. They're like a match when you light it in the dark."

Katie smiled for a second then quickly looked unhappy. "I hate to go to the restaurant but it's my job."

"Your eyes must be gray."

"Sort of gray," she admitted, then said firmly, "Indeed, I must be going."

"Your hair's wavy, isn't it?"

Katie nodded. "If you have nothing to do, you could walk with me to Lushman's. It isn't so far.' '

"You really want to go?" Johnny asked, almost harshly.

"Of course not," Katie admitted, knowing that was the truth.

"What would happen if you didn't?"

"Nothing much, I guess."

"You wouldn't get fired?"

"Who gets fired in these days when they can't find any help anywhere?"

"If you go now, I won't see you again," Johnny concluded mournfully.

Hearing in words what she had been thinking made it more grim. Katie said, "I know." Then, suddenly smiling,

"Sometimes I play a game on my way to work. I call it 'If.' "

"I never played it," Johnny said. "I never even heard of it."

"Of course not. I made the game up. You pretend at a street corner that instead of going the way you have to go you just turn and go another way, so you can see what would happen if you didn't go where you had to."

"And what does happen?" Johnny asked, following with difficulty.

"You never find out," Katie explained seriously, "because you never go that way. You just imagine what would have happened. You keep going the way you have to go. You always do."

Johnny shook his head. "I don't know much about games. All I know is I've got to be back at five this afternoon."

"Would you like me to be with you today?"

"More than anything," Johnny answered with a rush.

Katie made a quick decision. "Then I'll pretend to go to work, and not go."

"Honest?" His smile was warm with gratitude. "Then we can be together all day and go anywhere."

"Anywhere," Katie said happily. The idea of a day without routine, a day for broad wandering, was like treasure suddenly uncovered.

The counterman sauntered up to the table. "I couldn't help hearing what you said. If you want my advice—"

"That we don't," Katie said curtly.

"When my girl and me get a free day we go look at some place to put roots down after the war's over," he continued, clearing away the coffee cups. "To get along in this world you gotta find a formula. Without a formula life's a continual aggravation. And a chicken farm's a good formula. That's what I'd look for."

Johnny turned on him suddenly. "Ever hear of coccidiosis?"

The counterman looked puzzled.

"Chicken farms, and he never heard of coxy," Johnny

said loftily. "That's what kills your birds. You stick to
restaurants—you don't have to feed and water them all
day long, then find them dead with their toes turned up
the next morning."

Katie looked at Johnny with deeper pride. "And he
knows what he's talking about too."

"I don't want to spend all my life making coffee."

"It's good coffee," Johnny assured him.

"It's not bad." Katie admitted. "But at Lushman's
Eighty-two—"

"Lushman's?" The counterman almost screamed it.
"What are you, a comparative shopper, maybe? We sell
Lushman's our grounds."

Katie stood up angrily. "Let's be going, Johnny." She
took his arm. "Countermen are all loony. Now I wouldn't
go back to be with Joe today. He's like that too."

The fog had lifted outside and the streaks of the day
showed gold. On the street were a few cars, a few people,
a screeching trolley. An Italian grocerman was sweeping
his sidewalk. At a saloon a man was bringing empty kegs
from the cellar. A thin blue stream of sailors headed
toward the Navy Yard, passing a brown trickle of work-
men coming from the night shift.

"It'll be a nice day sure," Katie said.

Johnny sniffed the air. "Clear weather too."

"Sailors know about weather and a lot of things, don't
they?"

"Sailors know a hell of a lot," Johnny said modestly,
"about a hell of a lot of things."

Katie held tighter to his arm. "I was proud when you
spoke up about chicken farms."

"I ought to know about them. I left one to go to sea."

They were walking up the street, toward the subways.
Katie asked, "Where do we go?"

Johnny answered promptly, "To Manhattan."

They went along in step. Almost to herself Katie said,
"The whole shining world and twelve hours belong to
us."

"Eleven hours," Johnny insisted, pushing his hat back

on his head. "The first thing I wanted to do ashore was meet a girl and that's done, but there are four things more. Maybe we can do those together."

"Anything." Katie's face shone with an open smile.

The light breeze carried sea odor. They went on rapidly as Katie liked to walk; she felt she was stepping into a fresh new world where everything, even Sands Street, was miraculously new.

"I like to walk," Johnny told her. "You don't know how good walking in a straight line for a long way feels for a change."

Katie understood. "On a ship it must be like walking from the serving counter to the dishrack a hundred times with side steps to the coffee urn."

Johnny agreed. "And people! You never get away from people on a ship."

"That's like Lushman's Eighty-two." Katie was delighted they had something in common.

Each minute now seemed to Katie like time compacted, each second pounded more tightly full of meaning, each breath drawn five times faster. And she knew that every second, every step, was being stored in the shining mirror of her memory.

A sailor passed by, grinning. "Hey, Mac, if you're winding up an evening, you're late."

"Just beginning a day," Johnny boasted.

The sailor held his head. "I wish I was!"

As they went on Johnny said, "Maybe it's because you're the first girl I've talked to in months, but it seems like I never met one I could talk to so easily before." When she only smiled he asked, "What are you thinking about?"

"About how wonderful it must be to be a sailor and see the ocean," Katie said simply.

Johnny admitted it was pretty good. "I come from South Dakota. Until I left there all I saw was plows and grass and sometimes fields so dry the dust came down like dirty snow."

"I'd even like to see South Dakota," Katie said dreamily. "My folks brought me from Ireland when I was a little girl. If you don't count that, I've never been anywhere except New York and Brooklyn and the times I used to go see my sister in Perth Amboy."

"I always said if I could get away from that South Dakota dust I'd never leave the sea again," Johnny said fiercely. "And I won't, never."

Katie looked wistfully disappointed. "Don't you want a home and kids?"

"What!" Johnny broke his steady stride. "God Almighty, no!"

"Why not?" Katie's voice wavered.

Johnny swung around so that he could face her. "That's what all dames are always asking all sailors. What can a wife or a home or kids do for a sailor?" When he saw the twisted look on Katie's face, a look that showed fear of having abruptly marred something, his voice softened. "Later, maybe, when I'm old, I'll find a wife and home and kids somewhere."

Afraid that the thin threads between them might snap, Katie drew back at once. "Oh, sure, sure, Johnny," she said with awkward carelessness, "a sailor can't have any worries."

Johnny nodded in a superior manner. "I guessed you'd understand." He added confidentially, "You know what sailors call getting married? 'Going off the deep end!' That's what they think of it."

At that moment, and him so cocksure, he was like such a boy that Katie could feel him touch the soft rounded tip of her heart. And his touch, she was sure, would stay there for a long, long time.

"Yes, sir!" Johnny said, about nothing in particular.

They went along in the freshening air eagerly, sure that each succeeding step would surely bring them to something gay, new, and wonderful.

"There was once a dame in Norfolk," Johnny said cheerfully, "who was crazy about me. Her name was Nellie. She was always asking me, 'What about a home and kids?' Every time I met her in a bar she kept asking.

After a while I thought she was serious. Then one night she invited me to her place and right then her husband walked in. Can you tie that?" His face showed his disgust. "She had a home and maybe kids all the time. You know what I did? I remembered her address and I told every sailor I knew, 'If you want a hell of a good time in Norfolk, go to 232 Borron Street and ask for Nellie.' Johnny laughed. "I bet she and her husband haven't had any peace since, with sailors banging on her door day and night."

Katie winced at the story. "How could you do a thing like that, Johnny?"

"In the Navy you got to be tough," Johnny said loftily. Then he took her hand and squeezed it to reassure her. "Served the dame right, didn't it, when she had one husband already. How many of those does one dame want?"

Katie could not smile. She still felt the story just did not go with that pleasant face and that boyish smile. She said absently, "I guess you're right, Johnny."

"Oh, sure," he answered, then changed the subject. "I'll tell you the second thing I want to do on shore today. It's something I dreamed about on shipboard. I once saw a movie with a fancy hotel, with everything swell, with a million waiters and things and awful fancy food. Well, since I won't be ashore this time long enough for dinner I want to eat breakfast at a joint like that."

"That sounds easy." Katie was amused at his determination.

"You know a place like that?"

"The Waldorf's like that. I was a chambermaid there once. I even cleaned up a bedroom after two movie stars were in it. It was a mess."

"No kidding?" Johnny was impressed. "Then you ought to know your way around the place. Let's go there." He noticed some doubt on Katie's face and said hastily, "And don't worry about the cost. I got five months' pay in my pocket."

"It's not that," Katie hesitated. "I'm not quite dressed—"

"The clothes I wear are good enough for any place,"
Johnny said carelessly, "and if they won't let you in, you
hide under my collar."

Katie laughed. "All right, let's go to the Waldorf."

A sailor and his girl passed by, walking hand in hand in
slow step toward the gate at the end of the street. Their
mutual world was only a few hundred yards more of
silence.

Johnny looked at them hastily and frowned. "That'll
be us, this afternoon."

"It's a long way off yet," Katie assured him quietly. It
seemed impossible that there had been long years when
she had not known Johnny; and just as impossible that
there would be an hour and they not together.

Just around the next corner was the subway entrance,
with a long flight of steps to the platform below. The first
commuters were already there, some sleepy, some propped
against posts with their tabloids. A couple of sailors were
stretched awkwardly on benches, like men on a long jour-
ney who could go no further. Johnny smiled at them. "In
the Navy you learn to sleep anywhere."

Katie nodded. "But they look like such kids when they
sleep."

Johnny ruffled at that. "You ought to see how those
kids handle a six-inch gun."

Katie agreed that that might be different. "There's
something about sailors I feel every time I see them and I
don't know what it is. I guess it's envy because they can
go away from everything. Nothing ever follows after
them."

"It isn't like that," Johnny said seriously. "You take lots
of things with you to sea. Sometimes on shipboard I even
remember about the way South Dakota smelled in the
spring, and how good it smelled."

"After the restaurant," Katie said with envy, "I can't
smell anything any more." That stirred up other memories. "And that's not all. After work voices go on saying
in my head, 'Side dish of string beans, Leave the carrots
off the goulash, Light coffee, Dark coffee—"

Johnny nodded absently. He looked up and down the platform and stopped at the mirror on a slot machine. He took a comb from his pocket to run through his hair. Then he replaced his hat, balancing it carefully on the dark wave over his forehead. It always seemed ready to fall, never quite falling. Then he pulled down his blue jumper and straightened his tie.

"Other things too," Katie said when Johnnie came back. "Like 'Danish pastry, no, change it to cherry tart, no, Miss, make it vanilla ice cream.' Customers drive you crazy sometimes."

Johnny was only half listening. He looked along the platform again. "I can't believe I'm here. That is what you dream of on ships, subways and things."

Katie said simply, "I dream about a place where there aren't any steam tables with hands reaching over them and voices yelling at you all at once."

"That's how you fall asleep at night," Johnny said obliquely, "when you're lying in the dark with a lot of other men. Of course, being inside the ship you feel pretty good, but every guy's dreaming about being on shore and you really feel pretty alone."

"It's like the restaurant," Katie answered, understanding. "Even in the busiest rush hour sometimes you can forget where you are and imagine you're somewhere else, until the smell of food brings you back."

The roar of a train filled the station. A few people left the crowded cars. Johnny had to stand close to Katie. When curves threw her against him he smiled and Katie smiled back. The firm hold of his hand on her arm was good.

Johnny was radiant. He read the car signs, looked at all the people, shouted things Katie could not hear, and stared out at each stop as eagerly as a child heading for a picnic. At one stop he said, "Never been in a subway before. It's swell, isn't it?"

At Eighth Avenue and Forty-second Street Katie said, "Here's where we get out."

They came up to the street, now crude and dirty in

the morning light. In its plain ugliness it resembled an unwashed bathtub with litter unremoved.

"Is Times Square around here?" Johnny asked, sounding ready for any disappointment.

"Right over there."

Johnny looked. "Can't see much there to dream about," he said. "Most sailors I know are always saying, 'Boy, I dreamed I was in Times Square last night.'"

"It looks better at night," Katie said almost pugnaciously, moved by some maternal reason to want Times Square to look good for him.

Across the street was the white front of a chain restaurant. When Katie noticed it she felt a twinge of conscience. At Lushman's Eighty-two Joe would be pretty busy now and probably cursing all women for Katie's absence. She told Johnny. "There's one of the restaurants like I work in."

"It looks clean."

She agreed. "They're particular about that. And they all smell clean. They must buy the smell by the gallon and spray it around at night."

"You'll forget the joint when we're eating in a swell hotel. How do we get there from here?"

"Walk or take a cab."

In answer Johnny stopped a cab. Katie told the driver, "To the Waldorf."

The driver turned halfway to grunt, "Huh! Are you sure they'll take you in, sister?"

Katie was instantly belligerent. "And what do you mean by that?"

"You and the sailor'd have better luck trying a hotel I know on Ninth Avenue."

Her temper went up like a draft-blown candle flame. "Listen, John Jerk Anthony, who'd be wanting advice from the likes of you?"

"Okeh, sister, okeh," the driver agreed, starting his motor, "but I'm telling you, you won't get a room at the Waldorf."

Johnny grinned proudly at her. "You certainly handled

him all right." He started to put his arm around her, re-considered, and settled back in the corner.

"Fresh men aren't so hard," Katie said, unveiling a great truth. "It's the ones who get slinky without first getting fresh that need handling. Besides, taxi drivers don't mean it. They just try to be helpful."

"I never had much to do with them. I never saw any taxis in South Dakota."

Katie said wistfully, "We could tell this one to drive out there."

Johnny shook his head. "I wouldn't do that, even to a taxi driver."

"Sometimes in the subway I wish the train would find a new way to go," Katie said dreamily. "It would be funny if you got on at Forty-second Street and the next stop wouldn't be Thirty-fourth as it always is but some place in Pittsburgh or maybe Chicago."

"I was in Chicago," Johnny answered with great superiority. "I never saw anything worth a damn there."

The taxi bumped along. Johnny's eyes were watching the streets outside, as eager as a child seeing fresh wonders.

The faces of people who scurry the streets at seven show no eagerness or freedom. Dawn for them is no rosy light but the clank of a steel bell. Katie knew their faces and looked at them now with pity; few of them ever roamed away for a whole full free day.

The taxi turned into Park Avenue and after a few minutes stopped at the hotel. "Here it is!" Katie said, remembering that she had never once gone in through the front entrance. She smiled. "Maybe the manager'll be here to welcome us!"

"He'd better be," Johnny said grimly, "and with flowers in his hand." With a firm hold on her arm Johnny led Katie through the open door and into the large lobby. The light was dim. It was cleaning time and the furniture was out of place.

"No manager," Katie said briskly. "He's probably still asleep."

"If I knew where he slept I'd get him up all right," Johnny grinned.

Near by Johnny saw several scrubwomen busy with mops and buckets. "Makes me feel I'm still on shipboard to see all that swabbing down, although by this time we'd have the job done."

Katie glanced at the women. Her eyebrows rose, then her smile widened. "Look, there's Mrs. O'Geoghan, a friend of mine."

One of the women, the largest and the fattest, saw Katie. Her mouth dropped, then she came forward, waddling on fat ankles. She wore what looked like a long, flowing washcloth. Her mop was a hairy scepter in her hand. Her hair more or less resembled the mop in color and kink.

"Mrs. O'Geoghan was here when I worked here," Katie explained. "She was one of the eighteenth-floor cleaners."

"Katie Morrison!" Mrs. O'Geoghan smiled a full gold-toothed smile. "A soft sight for blistering sore eyes." She moved the mop from one hand to the other. "And would this fine lad be your husband?"

Katie looked proud. "This is my friend Johnny."

"A finer husband than a sailor no one'll be wanting," Mrs. O'Geoghan insisted, grinning at him. "They're always away, which is where husbands are better off."

Katie told Johnny, "Mrs. O'Geoghan was married three times."

"And three times widowed by the kindness of a beneficent God!" She added reverently, "And five sons, all in the Navy, God guard them." Then to Johnny, "Perhaps you'd be knowing Dennis, Patrick, Michael, Francis, and Liffey O'Geoghan?"

Johnny shook his head. "What was that last name?"

"Liffey, and like his old man, no one his equal for his eloquence. He can talk the ears off a bawdy goat. I named him Liffey after the river his old man drowned in. I felt I should do something to honor his passing, God rest his soul, and I wouldn't have said that at the time, which only shows how life has broadened my mind as well as my bottom." She turned to Katie. "You promised to come calling on me, Katie, and me having all the gossip of this whole bloody hotel stored up for years to tell you, and living only around the corner from you in Brooklyn."

"I know, Mrs. O'Geoghan."

"You can see with your own eyes I've been promoted," Mrs. O'Geoghan's large face glowed with pride, "from the eighteenth floor to the main lobby."

"That's fine," Katie answered warmly.

"Remember Mrs. Potocki, her who we called Webfoot? She who was always bedeviling me for leaving my mops damp? I left her behind on the eighteenth floor," Mrs. O'Geoghan continued, laughing so loudly that a desk clerk a short distance off looked up and frowned. Mrs. O'Geoghan frowned back, then lowered her voice. "When you step up to register, Katie, be sure to tell them you're married. They won't ask you to prove it but they're awful strict in this dump. That's the world, always lonely and inconvenient for lovers."

Johnny blinked and Katie smiled. "We just came in for breakfast."

Mrs. O'Geoghan looked skeptical. "Only breakfast, with a fine-looking young man like that?" She shook her head. "When I had young men like that I needed breakfast but afterward, and no pot of tea and bowl of porridge either, but steak and six bottles of stout. Then I was all ready for another day!" Mop and hair moved in time to her laughter. She saw that Johnny was slightly impatient. "I'll be getting back to my scrubbing," she said. "Young man, you'll not be finding any finer girls than the Irish, so don't be looking. And there's no finer than Katie Morrison you'd find among them if you searched through County Clare, County Limerick, and along Third Avenue here, which is where all the folk from Clare and Limerick have come."

Katie looked flustered. "Johnny and me are only friends."

"You come and tell me about him and I'll tell you how to change that," Mrs. O'Geoghan said. "Remember he'll be gone like all sailors and leave you desolated. And when sailors are gone it's only to other women their women can turn in their bottomless misery."

For a moment Katie thought of the evening of this very day, when Johnny would be gone, and of the emptiness unbearable. "If you're home tonight, I might come then."

"Come when you will, Katie, and God bless you both." She took Johnny by the arm and whispered, "If you don't know anything about the Irish, let me tell you something —when they say 'No,' what they usually mean then is that they're open to persuasion and hoping for it."

As Johnny led Katie through the lobby he said, "I never met anyone like that before."

"She's the kindest lady in the world. When I worked here she was like a mother."

"I'll bet. She even looks like a mother." Then Johnny looked around the still empty lobby. "A hell of a lot of deck here for old ladies like that to swab down."

"Wait till you see the size of the dining room," Katie promised, hoping it would be open. But first she stopped to use compact and lipstick and to straighten her gray jacket.

"Come on," Johnny said, impatiently, "you look swell!"

The room was open but without customers. One waiter was setting tables. The curtains were drawn and the light was poor. Johnny stopped at the doorway, fully impressed. He grunted, "Looks like the hangar deck on a carrier."

The waiter, a small man with gray hair and bushy black eyebrows, came to them, bowing and smiling.

Johnny said, "We want the swellest breakfast you can toss up."

"Certainly," the waiter smiled. "This way, madam."

"Did you hear what he just called you—madam?" Johnny asked in an angry whisper.

"He's just being awful polite."

Johnny shook his head. "It isn't a polite word in Norfolk."

They were seated at a table by a window. The waiter opened the curtains and left them. Johnny ran his comb through his hair, lit a cigarette, and settled back in his chair, while Katie again used lipstick and compact and patted down a stray fold of her blond hair. Johnny carefully inspected ceiling, walls, fixtures, curtains, and carpets. They satisfied him. "This is just the way I dreamed about it, and with a girl just like you across the table."

Katie smiled at him. The table, the linen, the carpeted quietness, and the broad earthy face of Johnny, so alive and so near, reminded her of the times she had sat at a table without Johnny, a whole life of such times—grabbing a quick meal in a corner at Lushman's, eating delicatessen food with her sister in a kitchen in Perth Amboy, with the sound of plumbing leaking in the hallway outside, or eating with a girl friend at a Chinese restaurant on Atlantic Avenue in Brooklyn, with the mystery of eating unknown foods in half darkness and the suspicion that, if the lights went on full strength, romance at sixty-five cents a plate would turn out to be boiled onion slices and stewed celery.

This was different, even to the feel of the heavy napkin spread on her lap. And Johnny was having a good time too, although he said little. Having him so happy, so wide-eyed, made her feel this new world was in a way hers and that she was guiding him, an eager stranger, through it.

The waiter brought menus and stood by, pencil in hand. Johnny took one look and whistled. "This place has a lot of grub. Must have ice boxes like a battleship's." He ran a finger down the menu. "Bring everything that's on here."

"Johnny!"

The waiter was undisturbed. "Would you like one or two portions?"

"We can't eat all that," Katie said sternly.

"But I said I wanted the biggest breakfast—"

"Then order everything you wouldn't get on shipboard."

That made sense. "Let's see—chicken liver omelette, Virginia ham, popovers—what are they?—creamed kidneys—"

The waiter was writing busily, a satisfied smile on his face.

"Total it up at once," Johnny ordered. "Does it come to more than thirteen dollars?"

"It's nearer fifteen."

"Good! That's swell!" Johnny grinned, not explaining why he was so pleased.

"If you don't mind my suggesting," the waiter began, "for a wedding breakfast—"

"Who said this was a wedding breakfast?" Johnny snapped. He even glared at Katie. "Why does everybody think we're married?"

"Must be the time of day."

The waiter agreed. "And the look on your faces."

"Well, we're not married," Johnny said petulantly. "And I'll tell you something—any time you see a sailor with a girl the chances are they aren't married. Or if he is, it's not his wife."

As Johnny was about to put the menu down he asked, "Don't you have any muskrat?"

"I beg your pardon?"

Katie was wide-eyed. "Who ever heard of anyone eating that, let alone for breakfast?"

"It's mighty good, rolled in flour and fried," Johnny explained with a flashing grin. "I thought a place like this would have everything."

The waiter, expressionless, said, "I'll ask the chef."

"Okay," Johnny agreed. "Tell him if he'll keep a stock on hand we'll always eat breakfast here every time I'm in town. Won't we, Katie?"

She nodded, laughing, "Even without muskrat."

The waiter went to the kitchen. Johnny said reminiscently, "We used to eat muskrat in South Dakota."

"I never heard of such a thing."

"Boy, you got lots to find out about me, baby," Johnny said. "You got lots to learn."

"I'm eager to," Katie said frankly.

Johnny laughed. Once more he combed his hair, lit a cigarette, and seemed to expand in his chair. And for a long time he said nothing, but took in luxury and novelty in pore and breath.

Katie looked at him and caught the warmth that was in him. One thing she already knew: this was the sort of man she could spend a life with, a life measured by short days and years too brief. This was the sort of man she could wait for at dark and rouse in the morning, the man for whom she was willing to cook and sew, and watch and worry over, work for, work with, and be jealous of. For such a man she could bear children gladly, sweat, and drive her nails into her palms. Life always has the problem of finding the right person to live with. Too many people compromise on the almost right, marry, then settle into bored silence and never satisfied desire. Now, for the first time in her life, Katie knew what she wanted, knew that she wanted it, and she was grateful to Johnny for the knowing. With that came sudden hunger for things she never knew before that she wanted.

Johnny was looking hard at her. "You're awful pretty, Katie. You don't look twenty."

"When I was a kid I used to play at being different ages. I could make myself up to look even as old as thirty. Sometimes age is just the way you wear your hair."

"You look pretty young at twenty," Johnny insisted.

Katie said, "My folks were Irish, straight Irish, from County Galway. All Irish women look young for a while. Then, all at once, they look old."

"I don't think I'll ever be old," Johnny said. "It's all in the way you think."

"Sometimes I feel so old I couldn't be older. Being old's all in the way you feel too." Then Katie smiled. "But not this morning, and, look, I'm glad I don't have to carry trays like this one."

The waiter arrived with a tray heaped with dishes topped with heavy silver covers. "Had to keep the chef out of the dining room by force," he said. "He wanted to shake the hand of any man who'd order a real old-fashioned breakfast." He began to take off the dish covers. "Shall I serve the dishes separately?"

"All together," Johnny commanded. "Just put 'em around the table."

When the dishes were spread out and the waiter had returned for another load, Johnny looked at the surrounding platters. "You don't get it this way in the Navy. They dip it out to you. And you never see food like this except maybe in the captain's quarters and I never ate there."

Katie pitied all captains for overlooking the most delightful breakfast companion to be met anywhere.

The way Johnny ate left no chance for conversation. The only thing Katie said was, "It's wonderful not to have to smell all this food being cooked."

As Johnny poured a second cup of coffee and scraped the dish of chicken livers clean he said proudly, "I got the record on our ship for eating most."

"That's a good record to have."

"Yep," Johnny agreed with full mouth. "I got a lot of records on our ship."

Katie gestured to the one ribbon on his chest. "Is this ribbon for one of them?"

Johnny looked surprised. "Don't you know what it's for?"

Katie shook her head. "Tell me."

Johnny hesitated as he pointed to a multicolored ribbon. "It's for lifesaving."

Katie looked proud. "I was sure it was for something like that. How'd you win it?"

"Nothing much," Johnny said, taking the last popover. "One of our ensigns fell overboard one day. I dived over the side and pulled him out."

"Oh, Johnny!" Katie was wide-eyed. "And all they gave you was that little piece of ribbon?"

Johnny shrugged his shoulders. "That's all ensigns are worth."

Katie looked troubled and curious. "I wish I knew about the Navy, about the way you live. I don't even know what you're on."

"Well"—Johnny finished his coffee first—"to anyone

who asks we're told to say, 'I'm on the U.S.S. None-of-your goddam-business.' "

"I didn't ask what its name was." Katie let a good Irish temper flare faintly. "I know enough not to ask. But I was just wondering about your life and what you do."

"Most of what we do is under what they call security," Johnny said sternly. "That means it's secret." There were some creamed kidneys left and he reached for them.

Katie looked skeptical. "Including where you sleep, what time you get up, what you do when you're free? After you're gone I want to be able to imagine where you are and what you're doing."

That impressed him. He answered, "I sleep on a bunk let down from one of the bulkheads. I get up depending on what watch it is, midnight or maybe noon, and when I have nothing to do, I do nothing. Just sit and talk and smoke or walk around and wish I was on shore. Sometimes we have classes to help get higher ratings."

The waiter returned with another full tray. "Hope you're still hungry."

"Doing all right," Johnny said.

He got a second breath and started on the new round of dishes. Katie stopped long before he did, but he finally broke down and had to give up. Then he looked over the table. "Anyway," he said, "I know now what fifteen dollars worth of food is. It's enough to make you awful sick of food."

He reached in his jumper pocket for his cigarettes. After lighting one he replaced the pack, carefully tucking in the paper ends. On second thought he began digging deeper in the pocket. With a satisfied smile he brought out a little paper-wrapped object. He opened it carefully in the palm of his hand, then held up a little round metal object. He said carelessly, "Here's a souvenir."

"What is it?"

"I don't know. I got it in Belfast when we put in there. That's in North Ireland."

Katie snorted. "The Six Counties, you mean. And they ought to be part of the Free State."

"From the way some people there talked you'd think they want to tow their island across the Atlantic and anchor it just off Boston," Johnny said. He handed the object to Katie. "I'm always bringing back souvenirs. Last time I brought back a coconut carved like a face so real you'd have thought it was human. I gave it to a bartender in Norfolk. You want this?"

"If you'd like me to have it," Katie said eagerly. She held the little object tenderly.

Johnny said wistfully, "I don't have anybody to give souvenirs to, and that's most of the fun bringing them back. I wish you could see what's in my locker aboard ship. I got a stuffed flying fish, a pair of slippers they call alpargatas—"

"What do you suppose this is?"

Johnny shook his head. "A medal or a coin or something like that. I got it in a store in Belfast, sort of a secondhand junk store. There wasn't much to buy in Belfast so I bought that. The storekeeper said it was a lucky medal." Johnny added reminiscently, "Belfast's an awful place. They had no souvenirs to sell at all."

Katie looked at it carefully. It was so worn that it was difficult to see what was stamped on it. On one side was a worn image of a stone monument, with lettering around it in an alphabet she did not know. On the other side was a man's face and more strange lettering. "It looks Irish," she said. "I mean, like an old Irish coin my old man used to have. He said it was lucky too, but I never heard of any luck chasing him."

Johnny added, "The storekeeper said it was silver."

"I don't care what it is. I like it." Katie put it carefully in her bag. When Johnny was gone she could touch this and know that her memories were real, that there had been a Johnny and she with him.

The waiter returned from the kitchen and asked, surprised, "Finished?"

"All we could eat."

"You certainly did a good job."

Johnny took the compliment modestly. "Let me have

the check." As he paid it he said, satisfied, "Now bring back the check receipted."

The waiter went off as Katie said, "That's a pretty expensive breakfast."

Johnny was delighted at something. "That will fix Lardlips good and proper."

"What's he got to do with it?"

"Well, you see," Johnny began boyishly, "he's always talking about the time he spent thirteen dollars for dinner at some swell joint in Frisco. You might think it entitles him to be an admiral, the way he talks about it."

"Sometimes when you talk about Lardlips you sound as if you really admired him," Katie said.

"That fat lunk?" Johnny brushed that aside. "Hell, no. Yet you got to hand it to him—he knows a hell of a lot."

"What about?"

"Oh," Johnny answered vaguely, "about lots of different things." Then he laughed gaily and his laughter, as so often, was like a child's. "Just wait till I get back and show him a check for fifteen dollars just for breakfast!" And Johnny looked as triumphant as he sounded, and Katie was pleased because he was so pleased.

Johnny pushed himself away from the table.

"Well, that's that. Now there are three more things I want to do."

"I remember," Katie nodded. "You're going to tell them to me one at a time?"

"One at a time."

"Then what's next?"

Johnny considered for a moment. "Where's Broadway from here?"

"Not so far, but it's not very exciting at this time of day. We crossed it coming here."

"I missed it, and I want to see it."

Katie agreed as she reached in her bag for a lipstick. She brought it out and the Irish medal with it. She looked at that for a moment and smiled. "I'm awfully glad to have this."

"Whatever it's supposed to be, I'll bet it isn't. You'd

think a place would have better souvenirs than that Belfast."

"I'm glad for it anyway." Then she glanced out of the window. "Oh, Johnny," her voice broke in a little gasp, "look, it's raining."

Johnny considered the rain and the sudden gray and judged them expertly. "It looks to me like an all day rain."

Katie frowned and her heavy lashes shadowed her eyes. "I wanted this day to be fair and sunny."

Johnny scoffed, "What's a little rain, with me a sailor?"

"I wish it would stop," Katie said sincerely. "Don't you?"

"Sure I wish it. We got lots of things to do." Absently he brought out his comb again and ran it through his hair.

At that moment a blade of sunlight cut through the gray. The rain turned iridescent for a moment, then became a spatter of fine drops.

"Look," Katie said, delighted, "we wished it and it happened."

Johnny nodded. "It would probably have stopped anyway."

Katie sat back and relaxed. "It's wonderful to have a day when it really matters if it rains. Most days don't make any difference to me, no matter what it does."

"Nothing to worry about all day," Johnny assured her. "I can take care of the weather personally."

The waiter returned with the receipted check. Johnny slipped it carefully into his hip pocket. "Good-by, sailor," the waiter said. "Come back when you're really hungry."

Johnny grinned. "Back in an hour or so." As he left the room with Katie he said, "That was even better than I dreamed it would be." He added in confidence, "Everything so far's better than I dreamed it would be and I've been dreaming it five months. A five-month dream is a hell of a long dream."

Outside the morning had freshened. The sky overhead was pearl gray now, its iridescence a promise of radiance and heat. Johnny breathed deep. "It's so fresh, it's like standing at the bow of my ship. Now, where's Broadway? Do we take a taxi?"

"Not unless you're in a hurry," Katie said. "It's not far and it's such a lovely morning."

Johnny took Katie's arm and they started across town. Katie glanced down to the Grand Central clock. It was just eight. Hours lay ahead. This was a morning to remember among the few other bright mornings of her life. Step by step as they went along, Katie recalled each single fact she knew about Johnny, reviewing each separate picture of him stored in her mind, remembering the fine firmness of his face, the youthfulness of his laughter, the promising warmth of his hand, the swing of all that was wonderful and free in his walk.

It was easy to imagine that it was peacetime again and they were walking to work, to separate for a few hours, that would make meeting at night the more exciting. It would be hard to leave Johnny at any time but it would be less hard with the close-fitting certainty of meeting him at the end of each long day and of being with him through each short night.

People moved fast around them now, all scurrying to some familiar weary destination. Their faces were as expressionless as burned-out electric light bulbs. Katie could smile broadly into the morning, even while she wondered if she went to work on other mornings looking as harried as these people. She probably did, but she could continue to smile; ahead of her today was time to spend with Johnny as she pleased, unlike the less happy or all unhappy people for whom hours, days, and even years could pass without even a faint touch of living pulse in them.

Deep in his own thoughts, Johnny began to think them aloud. "Funny that waiter should have thought we were married. Boy, he certainly doesn't know much about sailors."

Almost timidly Katie asked, "Why do you talk about avoiding marriage?"

"Any man does," Johnny said, "so he can show he's smarter than dames."

"That doesn't sound much like you," Katie said. It didn't. Even his voice was different, tinged with unpleasant harshness.

"It doesn't sound like me?" He seemed honestly surprised. Then, after thinking, he continued, "It's me! The reason sailors feel the way they do about marriage is because of the way dames are. They think their husbands ought to be like kids, a part of them, like they gave birth to the husband too. A man's got to feel free and women don't want that."

"Do you think all women are like that?"

"All I ever met or heard about," Johnny said positively. "They have to be. It's their nature."

Katie shook her head and said earnestly, "I think a wife could give her husband a splendid gift, Johnny, the sense of freedom. I think they could go on just as free as we feel now, walking along." When Johnny did not answer Katie asked, "Would you like that?"

He answered, "I like this, walking along with you now."

"You like me?"

"Sure. I knew that the first minute I heard your voice. You reminded me of my mother or maybe my wife—"

"Wife?" Katie knew her voice tightened.

"The one I'll marry some day when I'm old." He laughed, and Katie knew he had caught the concern in her voice. "Most sailors plan to settle down when they get old."

Katie wanted to ask, "Who wants them when they're old?" Instead she said, "Most of the fun in marriage is when you're young."

Johnny shook his head. "I know too many other things to do when I'm young."

Katie's red lips tightened ever so slightly but she did not answer. Before the hours ahead had passed she would have some chance to let him know how she felt.

Johnny was attracted by the shop windows on the crosstown street. He led her to a display of men's cloth-

ing. "Seems funny to look at those things," he said, "like
things belonging to another world. I can't even remember wearing civvies, and when I did I never had anything
like that." He pointed to a gray suit with green checks.
"I mostly wore overalls."

"I wish I could see you in that suit."

Johnny hesitated for a moment. "No, I'd look funny
in it." He grinned. "Besides, it costs seventy-five dollars,
Where I come from a man could dress up like a billboard
on that money. It'll be a long time before I dress like that
—maybe never."

"You won't stay in the Navy forever," Katie said, leading a question.

"I might want to," Johnny said. "That's another thing
women never understand, why men want to be sailors
and stay free." He waved at the people passing by. "Why
do the men all hurry like that? Because they're married,
most of them. If they weren't, with wives and babies and
rent to pay and clothes to buy, do you think they'd be up
so early hurrying like—like—"

"Like squirrels in cages?"

"That's it."

"Maybe they like it."

"Then they've never been sailors," Johnny said as final
argument.

So much of what he said, Katie decided, sounded as if
he were parroting someone. Perhaps he did think these
things and believed them profound. And perhaps he was
really not as young as he looked.

Now and then pretty girls passed, smart, fresh, and gay.
Johnny glanced at them now and then and whistled.
"Boy, there are lots of good-looking girls in America."

"Didn't you see any abroad, in Belfast?"

"All the good-looking Irish girls must have come to
America," he answered. "I'll tell you a funny thing. I was
going down a Belfast street with a friend of mine and he
said, 'Say, did you ever see so many Irish faces?'"

"What did he expect to see?"

"That's what I asked him," Johnny said, chuckling.

Now and then a passer-by turned to look at them, swinging along as fresh and unhurried as if they were part of the morning breeze.

"Is Broadway near Central Park?" Johnny asked.

Katie nodded. "Are we going there?"

"Yep."

"To row a boat?"

"Who rows boats?"

"All the sailors when they come to New York. They all go there."

"When I'm on land, I stay on land," Johnny said firmly. "I got other things to do in Central Park."

"I don't remember when I had nothing to do on a weekday at nine in the morning," Katie said gaily, the air of adventure still unbroken.

"On shipboard, time doesn't mean what it does on land," Johnny answered. "Sometimes I don't get to sleep until nine in the morning." He was suddenly thoughtful. "Today, though, time's different. If it's almost nine, that means I only have about eight hours more."

That went like a prow through Katie's gaiety. Those hours would end fast enough, dribbling away to the last second at the Sands Street gate. The last seconds would be bad, strained beyond reach of words. The hours immediately after, still bearing the freshest imprint of his presence, would be worse. But no hours, neither those of tomorrow nor the hours of a year yet to come, would ever be the same. Johnny would be in them, in anxiety, in hope, forever more a part of her though they never met again.

Ahead was Broadway. Katie said so. Johnny quickened his step but stopped abruptly at the corner, completely dissatisfied.

"Jeez," he said, "it looks crummy."

The street was not pretty. It looked like a dirty room with the bed not made and towels and newspapers crumpled everywhere around. A couple of old women were scuffing along to their morning coffee at the drugstore. One was dragging a mussy Pekinese, eczema and all. Three taxi drivers, with dirty shirts open against the promised heat, stood on the corner arguing. A few blowzy girls, in light coats and slacks, hurried on to some rehearsal or practice.

Johnny was puzzled. "I heard so much about it from Lardlips, I don't know what I expected to find. I guess he was just lying. It looks just like a harbor after a fleet's thrown the refuse overboard."

"Maybe it'll be better this afternoon." Katie did not know how to handle his disappointment.

"Lardlips said it was full of soft lights and beautiful dolls—he calls dames dolls—any time of the day or night."

Katie smiled. "Maybe he sees things differently."

"I don't know," Johnny said, "but he knows a lot about a lot of things and generally he's right. Particularly about women. The only trouble is, he's always blowing about that."

For a few minutes they stood on the corner while Johnny looked up and down the slattern street.

"Anywhere you want to go especially?" Katie asked.

"Let's just walk along. At least I can say I did that, and when I see Lardlips—!"

The air brought the mixed essence of shoe polish, worn rubber, orange peels, frankfurters, synthetic pineapple, and the morning smell of bars. Johnny sniffed. "One thing, it certainly smells different from the ocean."

"Even with all the fish dead, the ocean couldn't smell worse," Katie agreed.

They passed a souvenir store. Johnny led Katie to the window to look at a grimy display of sofa pillows, dolls, jewelry guaranteed ten carat plate, phonograph records, and plastic gadgets. He said, "I'll buy you anything you want."

She shook her head. "There's nothing I want."

Johnny looked surprised. "I thought dames always wanted things."

"You can't buy in stores what some women want," Katie said quietly.

Johnny considered that in silence as they walked along.

Then, suddenly, with a little bleat, he said, "There's something I want." He pointed to a shop with a sign, "Art photographs taken while you wait."

He led her to it. "I heard these stores were on Broadway. I hope this place is open. I'd like to have our pictures taken." He smiled to himself at some secret realization.

Katie asked no questions about the sudden wish for photography, but she was pleased at the promise of a picture with him.

The store was open. A little half-bald man, with a threadbare halo of hair around his scalp, put aside his newspaper as they entered. In suspenders and shirt open at the collar he resembled the keeper of some village emporium. He greeted them like old friends, with a shiny store smile. "Porkel's my name—at your service. First customers of the day—I always bring them luck. Wedding photographs, I hope?"

Johnny glared at him as if to ask, "Does everyone in New York City talk weddings and marriage?" He said firmly, "I just want to be photographed with my girl friend."

"Engaged, I hope?"

"No," Katie replied, no less firmly, lest Johnny get concerned.

"Too bad." Porkel shook his head. "The world is made for lovers. Rather, lovers are the only people really happy in it." He moved leisurely to a large old-fashioned portrait camera. "Too blind to see its sordid side, I suppose." He eyed Katie pleasantly. "I must say, you're a handsome exception to my usual run of first customers. Usually when any people turn up at this early hour they seem so gruesome I wonder why they want to be pictured for posterity as they looked at nine o'clock on a summer morning."

"If they pay for it, what of it?" Johnny asked.

Porkel shrugged his shoulders. "Because at heart I am an artist." He walked to a blank wall at the rear of the store. Overhead were some canvases on rollers. "You folks want any special background?"

Johnny did not understand.

Porkel pulled down from a roller a painting of a western scene, with mountains in the rear, a corral fence in the foreground, and an assortment of steer bones and saddles strewn everywhere.

"Not that one," Johnny said, and Katie was glad.

Porkel pulled down a scene on shipboard, with superstructure in the rear and the muzzles of large guns pointing into the foreground.

Johnny liked that but shook his head. "That's the one I'd use if I was alone, but it wouldn't look right with a girl. No one ever saw a woman on a battleship forward deck." He added generously. "That's a swell picture, though. Looks almost real."

"They're very fine paintings," Porkel admitted. "I did them myself."

Johnny drew back, impressed. "I never met but one artist before. He was a shipmate. But all he draws are naked women."

Porkel nodded. "Commonest form of marine art." He said reminiscently, "Yes, sir, once I was an artist. I began doing pictures on the mirrors of saloons, but Prohibition ruined me."

"Prohibition was a long time ago," Johnny remembered.

"I was ruined a long time ago," Porkel answered simply.

He rolled down a Hawaiian background, with tropic moon and ragged palms. "Sailors go for this one, Mac, particularly at night when I keep a few girls around here for camera companions."

"Camera companions?" Katie asked skeptically.

"Sure," Porkel said. "Lots of sailors want to be photographed with a girl so they can send the picture back home and make their home-town girl jealous."

For a moment Katie wondered whether that was Johnny's motive in being here now.

Johnny asked, "Haven't you anything from New York City?"

"Ah, a realist!" Porkel exclaimed as he unrolled a picture of the skyline.

That pleased Johnny. "Let's go. Is that all right, Katie?"

She nodded.

"It's too bad he hasn't got a picture of the front of Lushman's Eighty-two."

Porkel stood them as he wanted. He fiddled with the lights, then stepped back and stared through the ground glass. He looked up with clear satisfaction. "Young lady, your hair is lovely enough but you have a look in your eyes—if I could catch it in a picture we'd both be famous."

Katie did not know if he was serious but she was happy to see that Johnny was impressed. With the air of an expert he said, "That's what I've been telling her."

"And if a woman ever looked at me like that—!" Porkel returned to his ground glass.

Katie smiled up at Johnny proudly. Then she said, "Wait a minute. Your hat isn't on right." She altered it a trifle.

Porkel emerged again, shaking his head. "There's a woman—no man is good enough. She has to start improving him."

"Indeed, and most men need it!"

Porkel laughed at that. "If I were you, I'd marry her, Mac."

As Johnny frowned awkwardly, Katie felt sorry for his embarrassment.

"Now then!" Porkel had his camera ready. "No, stand closer. 'Fraid of her, sailor?"

"No, sir!" Johnny awkwardly put his arm around Katie.

The touch of his arm on her shoulders was a soft but firm and warm push on her heart, driving her blood with a spurt. She tried to smile, hoping her face did not show what she felt.

"Perfect!" Porkel looked pleased. With automatic skill he slipped plates in the camera and took one, two, three pictures. "There," he said, with surprising relief, "all beautiful. If you were married, your children would prize them."

Johnny stepped forward, his shoulders high. "Mister, everywhere I go today everyone talks about marriages and getting married. Why?"

Not familiar with all the expressions on Johnny's face, Katie was not sure what his heavy, almost belligerent, look meant.

Whatever it meant, Porkel smiled at it. "You think I'm only a Broadway tintyper, sailor? In a way, that's a side-line here. I guess you'd call my real business being a middleman in romance."

"What's that?" Johnny sounded interested immediately. Katie beside him was just as interested.

Porkel carefully brushed the front of his shirt with his finger tips. "You'd be surprised how many people need help in romance. Well, I help 'em."

Johnny asked suspiciously, "What kind of help?"

"Sometimes it's a ring or a dress suit or maybe a best man for a last minute wedding, any time of day or night. Sometimes they want to get married in a hell of a hurry and we got a three-day law in New York State, with blood tests. It takes the Mayor trying to be cute and some tabloid trying to up its circulation to get the law set aside."

"Why can't people wait three days?" Johnny asked.

"You'd be surprised how many couples, just like you, go walking along Broadway on a nice summer evening looking for fun, without a thought in their heads. Then, pouff, they decide the best fun they could have would be to get married and they want to get married, just like that. No fever's worse than wanting to get married in a hurry and not being able to. It does things to you, sailor. Maybe the guy's leave ends in a couple of hours. Maybe it's four aye em. Where would you get married in New York City at that hour?"

"Damn if I know," Johnny admitted, "but if I wanted to get married that bad, which I never would, I'd find a way somehow."

"Sure you would," Porkel agreed generously, "and if

you were in New York City you'd come to me, and you'd
be smart. I'm open all night. Me and my partner's got
everything worked out and waiting—a taxi to Jersey
where you can get married right away, a license, a min-
ister, priest, or rabbi, a taxi back to New York, two hours
or as many as you want in a special hotel, and a taxi
waiting at the hotel door for the railroad station if you're
in that much of a hurry. We can wrap up a wedding complete in three hours and we haven't had one failure yet."

"You mean, no divorces?" Katie asked.

Porkel shook his head. "I mean, we never yet missed
getting the bridegroom on the train he had to make." He
continued proudly, "We got everything down to a system,
different prices for different purses. Twenty-five, fifty, a
hundred, and two hundred dollars. The last includes a
real lace wedding dress—I got a closet full of 'em—a hotel
room with a view of the Hudson, and a bottle of cham-
pagne, American, but the best we can get."

Johnny was listening closely, now wide-mouthed.

"We take an interest in our clients," Porkel insisted.
"Some are so pleased they come back a second time or
more, with another guy, of course. One dame's been married four times by us."

"Without divorcing?"

Porkel shrugged his shoulders. "I don't ask."

Johnny was indignant. "Allotment widows!"

"Maybe," Porkel admitted. "There's a lot of 'em
around." Then, casually, he added, "You folks sure you're
not interested?"

"No," Johnny snapped. His face was as firm as his voice.

"Too bad," Porkel said carelessly. He smiled. "We do
lots of other things too, all in the romance business. A
marine fell for a chorus girl in *Here Come the Girls.*"
Porkel lit a cigarette. "That was easy. We fixed up an
introduction and damn if they didn't get married a week
later. A two hundred dollar job too."

Katie was watching Johnny. He was staring like a gog-
gle-eyed fisherman trying to identify some new species.

Porkel remembered the plateholder under his arm. "I

better get to work on these myself," he said. "I was hoping my partner Hosenfenster would come along, but he seems to have disappeared." He added in confidence, "Hosie takes care of the Jersey end of our business and doubles in spare time in developing and retouching." He started toward a closet in the rear wall. "If any customers come, entertain 'em. If you can sell 'em a wedding, you get ten per cent."

He slammed the door shut behind him.

Johnny scratched his head. "New York has the damnedest people."

Katie agreed. "Isn't it fun?"

"It's wonderful I guess." Johnny was thoughtful. "I used to think all the screwballs were in the Navy. In spite of some of the ensigns we get, I guess we got no more than our share." He lit a cigarette. "One thing still puzzles me. Everywhere we go people talk about marrying."

"They talk about it all over the world," Katie said promptly.

The door opened in great haste. A small man, prematurely aged, came in. He wore an old brown coat, flabby pants, and a kicked around hat. He looked pale and worried, like an unemployed ghost. "Porkel!" he yelled. "Porkel!"

There was a muffled answer from the closet. A few seconds later Porkel appeared, just as the man was about to bang on the door.

"Hosie!" Porkel snapped. "What happened?"

Hosenfenster talked so fast, first from one side of his mouth, then from the other, that at first Johnny and Katie could scarcely catch separate words.

"It'samazinghorrifying," Hosie bolted. "Thecopwasallforgettinrough."

"Where were you when you phoned?"

"Over in Jersey," Hosie said, slowing down as he ran out of breath.

"Think he'll be here?"

Hosie nodded sadly. "It's a certainty."

Porkel explained to Johnny, "This is Hosenfenster, my assistant and partner."

"The mugg started fighting with the dame as soon as they left the parsonage," Hosie continued. "It was a situation."

"Yeah? What happened then?"

"So the guy says he wants his dough back—the marriage wasn't worth it. So he says either he fights me or the dame."

"So?"

"So I thought I could do the dame a favor and myself also, so I slugged him. But a cop saw me."

Katie glanced at Johnny and smiled to see how absorbed he was.

Porkel noticed it too. "Hosie, you're giving a bad impression to these people."

Hosie seemed to see Johnny and Katie for the first time.

"Customers? Porkel, I ain't going back to Jersey for no one until I've had a lot of coffee."

Porkel shook his head. "They aren't interested in marriage."

Hosie swung around pugnaciously as if something he valued had been challenged. "Who of you's hesitating? I got a lot of arguments for men, a lot of different ones for women."

"We only came in to get our pictures taken," Johnny told him curtly.

"You could still get married, couldn't you?" Hosie insisted. "Maybe this girl don't want to marry this fine boy?"

"That's it," Porkel said, "you persuade 'em. I got pictures to finish." He went back to the closet and closed the door.

Hosie continued, to Johnny. "Maybe you're already married. We had one sailor in here once who had five wives, a regular Sinbad of a sailor."

"Johnny's not that sort," Katie said stoutly.

"Besides, we've only known each other a couple of hours," Johnny added, his voice and his jaw hardening.

"Long enough," Hosie insisted. "Get to know your wife after you marry her. That way marriage is always full of surprises."

"Furthermore," Johnny continued, his voice as hard now as his jaw. "I'm not marrying anyone."

"My boy," Hosie said, his voice smooth as a gardenia, "think of coming back home to wife, home, fireplace, children. We can fix all that for you, all in one package, at a price to fit—"

Katie interrupted, "Your partner told us that, but we aren't interested."

Johnny looked at her gratefully, unwilling to admit he couldn't handle a situation but nonetheless grateful for help. And Katie wondered why she should be so glad at having helped him.

"No offense," Hosie said cheerfully. "No offense, none actually."

Porkel appeared again from the closet, a grin on his face. He had wet prints in his hand and displayed them proudly. "Masterpieces, each of them."

On all of them Katie's nose was too large, her cheeks too broad. But Johnny looked handsome and he was pleased. His sudden grin showed that.

Porkel nodded sadly to Katie. "Didn't catch that light in your eyes. The camera is really an insensitive automatic brute with mechanical limits. No soul."

Johnny had a request. "Will you please write on the back of each picture, the date, the time of the morning, and the place, then sign them?"

"Sure." Porkel hunted around for a pen. As he did so, Katie wondered why Johnny was so insistent.

Johnny put two pictures in his wallet and handed one to Katie. "You want this?"

"Oh, yes." Katie put the print in her pocketbook with greatest care.

Hosenfenster entered the closet to clean up.

Porkel happened to glance to the street. He whistled. "Hosie, take a look!"

Katie looked too and saw a large policeman outside,

obviously curious about the place and about to come in.

"Hosie," Porkel grunted, "there's Flitter again. He after you?"

"Who can tell what goes on in a cop's mind?" Hosie asked. "Besides, who can tell how rumor gets around? Maybe Flitter got a phone call from Jersey about this morning."

"Maybe," Porkel agreed nervously. "Maybe he's got nothing on his mind but a bald spot."

Katie did not like the sense of suspense and pulled slightly at Johnny to start him to the door. He stood rooted and would not move.

"You better head in the closet and sleep there," Porkel said, "because Flitter looks like he's camped outside for good."

Johnny was enjoying this. He whispered to Katie, "Boy, will I have a yarn to tell when I get back to the ship. Hey, here comes the cop and he looks like a line squall."

Flitter had made up his mind to come in. He entered heavy-footed and heavy-browed. "Hosenfenster around?"

Porkel nodded to the closet. "In there. Hey! Hosie! Guests!"

Katie whispered to Johnny. "I wish he'd let him alone."

"So do I!"

Hosie came out, a smile breaking on his face. "Patrolman Flitter, my old friend."

Flitter stood still, dark and angry. But to his anger was added something bewildering, and he said nothing.

"Something we can do for you?" Hosenfenster asked politely.

"No, I guess not," the policeman said vacantly. "I guess not."

Hosie and Porkel exchanged glances that dripped gratefulness for small miracles or at least changes of mind.

"Well, while you're here," Hosie said, "this gives us a chance to take your picture."

"Sure," Porkel added, taking a cue, "we've been wanting to do that for a long time." He jumped to his camera.

Hosie took Flitter by the arm and pushed him up against the backdrop.

Flitter, still looking bewildered, was muttering, "What the hell do I want with pictures!"

Porkel was already at work. "Hosie, we'll give him the best, the f 6.3 lens we use only for special customers. Nothing's too good for Flitter, not even panchromatic plates."

Johnny, who had watched without a word, began to look puzzled. Katie felt faintly uneasy and whispered to him, "Let's go."

He nodded and they started for the door quietly while Porkel was busy at the ground glass. Hosie, seeing them leaving, caught them at the door. "Remember, sailor, if you change your mind, we can do a hell of a good hitching job in three hours."

"Small chance," Johnny said.

"You're a lucky guy, having a nice girl," Hosie said still friendly. "But watch out for pickups—they're all only after allotments. Broadway black widows, we call 'em."

"Oh, sure," Johnny said carelessly. "G'bye."

Out on the sidewalk they went on for fifty feet before Katie said, "I don't know why, but I suddenly felt I had to get away from that place."

"The cop puzzled me." Johnny nodded wisely. "Men don't go around looking like that unless they're going to raise hell." He scratched his head and pushed his cap in place. "But he didn't do a damn thing, just look lost."

"It was funny."

"I guess he changed his mind, that's all." Then Johnny laughed. "Probably he saw your face and decided he had to act decent in front of a lady. You do look an awful lot like a lady. Even that picture shows it."

Katie laughed at that. "I don't know if I want to look like one. If you could see me at Lushman's!"

Johnny took the pictures from his pocket and examined them. "I'm awful glad I got these with the time of the morning written on them."

That still puzzled her. "Why?" she asked. "What does that matter?"

"It's something personal." Johnny put the prints back in his pocket. "Something between me and Lardlips." Then, triumphantly, "And getting this picture was the third thing I wanted to do ashore."

"Then I'm glad you got them." She fell in step with him. "But I'd like to know why." When he laughed at his own secret she felt all her earlier gaiety come back, borne light on the morning air. "What's the next thing we do, sailor?"

"You'll see soon enough." He held his little mysteries close. He looked up Broadway and saw the trees at Columbus Circle. "Where's Central Park?"

"Straight ahead." Katie was pleased afresh at his open eagerness.

The air was warm and brought the odor of a Broadway summer morning, compounded of many sleazy things. Johnny sniffed it. "It's good to smell something that doesn't smell like sea water."

Katie laughed at that as at the funniest thing she had ever heard.

"You mustn't laugh at the next thing we're going to do," Johnny warned her.

"I won't laugh." She was growing curious, trying to guess and getting nowhere.

"Promise?"

"Promise!"

They continued up Broadway and crossed the Circle. Then Katie said, "Here's the Park!"

"Yes, sir!" His face was all alight. "And here's one thing I've waited for a long time."

She saw such glowing happiness in his face that she felt her throat choke up. Then, with her own voice speaking and her own ears hearing, but without any conscious willing, she said, "Oh, Johnny, I love you."

But at that moment Johnny dashed ahead, into the Park, leaving her standing alone. Katie felt sheepishly ridiculous, not sure but that her impulse had frightened him away forever and that he would run without stopping. She went after him without hurrying. He had crossed the road and was on the lawn. Seeing him grinning from ear to ear, Katie felt a little more reassured.

When she joined him he almost shouted, "Look, grass!"

"What about it?"

"That's the fourth thing I wanted in New York." His face was radiant. "Just to touch grass. How much do you think you see on shipboard?"

Katie saw a new look on his face, of deep hunger deeply satisfied.

"Let's sit down." He did so at once. "My God, it feels good!" Then, with a flush of embarrassment he added, "Maybe you wouldn't understand."

"Sure I understand." Katie sat down. "Everybody wants to do something in life like feeling grass again, only a lot never get the chance."

Johnny settled back full length. "I even dreamed about it. It smells like South Dakota grass, though maybe not as good." He turned his face to the lawn. "There's something special about the way grass smells when the sun heats it up and the smell of the earth comes up through it."

"I guess so," Katie agreed slowly, "but if you live in the city you don't have much to do with grass."

Johnny straightened out again. "Mind if we stay here awhile?"

"Anywhere, all day, so long as I'm with you."

"You'll stay with me to the last minute."

Katie lay back beside him and the sun's heat blurted across her face. She wondered if Johnny had heard what she said at the entrance to the Park just before he bounded away. He was so intent on the grass that he had probably heard nothing. She decided not to chance asking about it.

The sun on her face felt good. Overhead the large white summer clouds were forming.

"Katie!" Johnny turned suddenly to her so that his lips were near her ear. "Do you?"

"Do I what?" she asked lazily.

"What you said as we came to the Park. Do you really?"

"Yes," Katie said, her voice suddenly trembling.

"Since when?"

"It seems like always."

For a moment Johnny said nothing and seemed awfully remote. Then, quick as a swooping bird, his whole body was close to her. "You know something, Katie? I love you too."

Katie had not expected to hear that. She glanced nervously at his face, so close to hers. What he was saying was there in his face.

"But maybe it's just for today," Johnny added, both as insurance and warning.

Katie laughed at that. "You've probably told that to lots of girls."

"Sure I have." As casually as possible and with a change of tone he added, "A sailor gets engaged to lots of girls. It's fun, as long as you're careful not to be the first guy around a girl—or the last."

Katie did not laugh at that. "When you talk that way, Johnny, it doesn't sound like you. It sounds like somebody else."

"It's me, all right," Johnny insisted, frowning.

When Katie saw the frown she said hastily, "But I love you anyway."

Johnny looked contented. "I feel so wonderful, like the way when you come on deck and it's been dark and stuffy down below and you walk right into a fresh wind."

"Uh huh." That summed up her whole day thus far. "You know, Johnny, you're different from so many fellows I know."

That struck a slight spark. "You know many?"

"Not many, and none just now. But with them it's horses or what's your favorite orchestra or did you see such and such a movie or how about coming to Manhattan Beach for a weekend—or other things."

"Uh huh."

"They don't know anything real to talk about."

"Yeah, sure." Then Johnny said absently, "If I was an admiral I'd keep a box of dirt somewhere on deck and plant it with grass."

"I'll bet you could be an admiral some day if you wanted to be."

Johnny laughed at that. "Jeez, women don't know a darn thing about the Navy."

Katie had become slowly conscious of Johnny's lithe body, close beside her. She asked curiously, "What's the fifth thing you came ashore to do?"

"Huh? What?" Johnny sat upright. "Oh, that." He smiled. "That can wait, I guess."

"What is it?" She was increasingly curious.

"I'll tell you later." He moved away and sank back on the grass.

On the lawn nearby a soldier and a girl were lying in close embrace, oblivious of passing baby carriages, nurses, taxis, pedestrians, and two boys trying to get a kite in the air. Johnny gestured to them with a nod of his head. "That must be what grass does."

"Or the summer and the touch of the sun."

"Yeah."

"Or being a boy and being a girl and being together."

"Yeah." He took her hand.

She moved closer to him. His hand went slowly through her hair. "You have lovely hair. It's so soft."

"It takes a wave nice," Katie answered, quivery at the touch of his fingers.

His hand slipped over her forehead. "Your skin's soft too."

"Isn't every girl's?" Katie laughed lightly. "What about all those girls in Ireland and everywhere else you've been?"

Johnny laughed nervously at that. His hand slipped over her eyes. "Your eyes are what I like most. I never saw that color before. They're like a cigarette lighter, when it works. I noticed them first time we sat in that Brooklyn restaurant. That seems long ago, doesn't it?"

"Awfully long ago." Katie's body quivered when his

hand rested and quivered more as it moved over her. When his hand came, slow as soft rain, over her face and reached her lips, she held it there and kissed it. "I don't feel like there'd ever be oceans between us again, Johnny, even if I know they're going to be. But maybe they won't be so wide." She smiled. "There's an old Irish proverb, 'No water is wide if a bridge be over it.' "

Johnny was following the track of his own thoughts. He said, "Sailors get lonely. I guess no one gets as lonely as a sailor."

"Except, maybe, the girl who wants the sailor."

They lay side by side, saying nothing else, needing nothing else to say. Johnny stroked her arm, then found her hand and did not let it go. The wind over the Park was warm, as gentle as the brush of soft lips.

Katie began to hum:

> "I know where I'm going,
> I know who's going with me,
> But, oh, the thing I don't know,
> Who is going to marry me?"

"That's a pretty song," Johnny said dreamily.

"It's Irish. I've forgotten most of it except the last line: 'My handsome winsome Johnny, maybe he will marry me.' " Not until the words were out did Katie realize that Johnny would think she was teasing him.

He swung himself up on one elbow. "Say, for the tenth time, why are dames always thinking about marriage? Lots of people get on good without it."

"It's the way women are, I guess."

"Dames will do funny things to get married." He laughed lightly at some memory. "A while back we were in Glasgow. There was a dame I was with most of the time we were there. Somehow she found out we were sailing and she locked up my clothes so I'd miss the ship. And she said she wouldn't give them back to me unless I promised to marry her in the morning."

"What did you do?" Katie asked because she felt she was supposed to ask.

"Told her I'd either break her door or her jaw—she could take her choice," Johnny said. "So she handed over the closet key."

Katie winced. "That doesn't sound like you."

"You said that a couple times before," Johnny answered. "It's me, all right."

The sun's heat was rising and its glare began to come through the mist. The air was as heavy as a hot damp towel. Katie put her hand up to shield her eyes. So many things about Johnny would take thinking over later. For the moment it was enough that he was here. She said quietly, "When you're indoors all morning you don't know the world outside's like this."

"Like this," Johnny agreed, moving closer to her.

Katie smiled at him. "You said you wanted to do five things on shore."

"I know," he said lazily. "There's one more."

"What do you want to do next?"

"We got time."

"No hints?"

Johnny laughed. "Maybe it's better without hints." He sat up suddenly. "Say, we don't have so much time after all, do we?"

"Not so much." Katie sat up and straightened her jacket. She was sure she could guess what Johnny wished. She looked at him and smiled. "With your hair mussed, you look like such a little boy. You'd never know you were twenty-four."

"Little boy!" Johnny sounded scornful. He took out his comb and worked vigorously on his hair. Then he stood up. "Come on, let's walk. I feel restless."

"Sure," Katie agreed, glad to match his moods.

After he helped her up they went lazily across the lawns, following one path, then another. The grass was just lightly spattered with people. "I've been here a couple of Sundays," Katie said, "and I never saw the Park as quiet as this."

"Here with other fellows?"

"Sometimes."

"Sailors?"

"You meet all kinds around a restaurant but none of them ever counted for much." When Johnny seemed satisfied Katie continued, "I always hoped I would know one sailor well."

"Do you mind them when they're fresh?"

"No one ever got fresh with me, Johnny," Katie said bluntly. Then she added, "Usually there are lots of them here in the Park, but this morning there don't seem to be any."

"Good!" Johnny said cheerfully. "I can get along without sailors for a while."

They crossed a road, hand in hand, and came to a descending path. It brought them to the pond near Fifty-ninth Street.

"Come on, Johnny," Katie said teasingly, "what's the next thing we do?"

He did not answer. He was looking straight ahead at the pond. Then, almost squealing with joy, he said, "Look, ducks! What are they doing in New York?"

"We got everything," Katie said with a sense of proprietorship.

"Pekins and Japanese wood ducks!" Johnny's face was glowing. "I'll bet not many people who come here can name the different kinds."

"I couldn't," Katie admitted frankly. "The only duck I know is the special that Lushman's serves with filling, two vegetables, apple sauce, bread and butter, ninety cents." She laughed. "And Lushman's can get eight serving from one duck."

"Hhm," Johnny grunted, "and the farmer was probably lucky to get sixty cents for it."

Johnny walked eagerly to the edge of the pond. Katie saw on his face the look she now knew and loved, of completely unpretended happiness, not the Johnny with his women in a dozen different seaports, but a simple forthright boy. "Back home we had a lot of ducks. The man I worked for was crazy about them." His face was shining, as if he had found old friends by chance. "He kept a lot of them. I used to have to feed them, the one job I really liked. They eat a hell of a lot." He smiled at her. "You want to know about ducks?"

"More than anything else in the world," Katie said gaily, "although I never knew I did until a minute ago."

Johnny took her arm and walked slowly along the edge of the pond. "Those white ones are Pekins, the best duck there is. Better than Indian Runners. Some of them get to be as big as swans." Johnny talked with unexpected strong feeling. "You know, once I used to dream about owning a duck farm all my own."

Katie had never imagined herself on a duck farm but now she tried. "Wouldn't a man need a wife on a duck farm?"

"A hired man would be better," Johnny said with authority. "Wet mash is awful heavy stuff for a woman to lug around."

Katie smiled and looked out across the pond. One particularly large white duck was swimming around in slow circles. She pointed to him. "I wish he'd come here."

"I wish so too," Johnny said, "but they never do come. Ducks are just stubborn."

The duck swam its slow circle then quietly turned and headed toward the shore.

"Look," Katie said, smiling, "he's coming!"

"Well, I'll be damned," Johnny answered, "that just goes to show you can't tell anything about a duck!"

The duck came straight to them, sniffing for food. When no odor pleased him he whisked his tail and quickly turned away, a little wake rippling behind.

"See, I can charm ducks," Katie said triumphantly. "Couldn't a woman take care of the baby ducks on a duck farm?"

"Ducks smell awful," Johnny said curtly, dismissing the whole idea. "A woman'd get fed up with them awful quick."

He turned away from the pond and Katie followed. Seeing an empty bench, he said, "Let's sit here awhile." His restlessness returned. He flipped away a cigarette and said slowly, "I could think of worse things than sitting here and watching ducks, but that seems like a hell of a way to spend a morning." He turned around to face Katie. "We haven't got so much time left."

"You said that."

"What do you think we could do?"

"I thought," Katie said carefully, sure that by his manner she had guessed, "that there was something you wanted to do particularly."

"Oh, sure, but you got any ideas?"

Johnny's vagueness made her less sure of her guess. Not knowing what to say she said, "We could go to Coney Island."

"What's the ocean there got that I haven't seen?"

Since Johnny was unwilling to help, Katie said, "There's one thing I'd really like to do."

"Tell me," Johnny said hopefully.

"I'd like to go see your boat."

"We call her a ship," Johnny said with professorial superiority and with some little disgust. He shook his head vigorously. "Nope." He said nothing for a moment while he hunted for words. Then, slowly and weightily, he began, "I'll tell you what I'd like to do." He seemed ready to start, but again he stopped while Katie waited, feeling the soft sun on her face like a warm intimate gesture. "I'll tell you." But first he took out his cigarettes, carefully chose one, examined the wrapper and both ends, then took a match card. He meticulously chose the proper match, looked to see how he was holding it, struck it, and lit the cigarette carefully. After making sure the cover was folded in, he read the printing on the cover as carefully as a proofreader, put the matches back in his pocket with caution, and slowly took a first puff of the cigarette.

"You see," he said, ready to make an important statement, "what the government ought to do, or maybe even these dames who are always passing out sandwiches and doughnuts to sailors, is to fix up a place where a sailor and his girl can be alone, particularly when a sailor has so little time ashore." He took a deep breath, looked at

Katie, saw nothing that alarmed him, and went ahead. "That's what I'd do if I was a civilian. In fact, if we had such places I'd even be willing to let soldiers in. They must feel like sailors do sometimes."

Katie was smiling now, sure she had jumped safely over a broad guess to a secret. But she asked innocently, "We're alone here, aren't we?"

"Oh, sure, yeah—" For a second he seemed helpless, then surrendered to helplessness and could not go on. He looked to Katie for help and saw only her warm smile. He misread it and quickly tamped out his cigarette. He nodded to the path in front of them. "Where does this go?"

"To the Zoo and then up to the lake where all the sailors go boating. I guess every sailor in New York shows up there sooner or later."

"Then let's walk, but in another direction." Johnny stood up quickly and quickly they started back into the Park.

A steady stream of baby carriages, toddlers, nurses, and small boys and girls was passing by. On a bench a perspiring mother was stripping her baby down to diaper and shoes.

"Look at that," Katie said enviously.

"You sound like you'd like to have one."

"I would. A whole house full!"

"Babies are no good," Johnny insisted. "I knew one once, a baby—I mean I lived in a house where there was one. They're just headaches. Diapers and bottles and all day long you have to be doing something for them. They're not like human beings who can take care of themselves. When they get a fever you get worried and then the fever goes away quick and you worry because it went away so quick. I know!" Then he laughed. "What the hell am I talking about babies for when I got lots more important things to talk about?" He saw an empty bench ahead. "Let's sit down again."

"Sure," Katie said, happy and amused.

Again Johnny took a deep breath. "I was talking about the fifth thing I wanted to do on shore."

"That's right," Katie agreed patiently.

"I always believed—well—usually, I always said that if you want anything from a dame, ask right out for it."

That did not sound like Johnny. But Katie said, "I wouldn't put it that way but maybe that's right."

"So," Johnny said, taking a cigarette again and lighting it quickly, "so—"

On the bench opposite a man saw Johnny with his cigarette. He came over quickly. "Could I trouble you for a light?"

He was a small man with a thin gray face and sharp close-set eyes. His clothes were those of a man who had slept in a mangle. His brown pants and coat were unpressed. His shirt looked as though it had been ironed by sticking it on a bar mirror. His tie was frayed at the knot and spotted on the way down. Yet there was something in his face that seemed to reach for sympathy beyond his shabby clothes. And his voice was soft, almost subservient, the voice of a man who expected that, no matter what he said, he would be kicked hard for it.

Johnny gave him a match and waited for him to go.

But the man said, "I'm always so glad to have a chance to talk with a sailor. May I sit down for a moment?"

"Well—" Johnny sounded irritated.

Katie looked at the man and saw something she liked in his face. She said, "Of course, if you wish. Isn't that so, Johnny?"

Johnny agreed, scowling at the fate that had turned up an interruption at just that moment.

"Name's Watson," the man stated. He puffed his cigarette slowly. "You see in front of you a man whose life was ruined by the Navy."

For just a second the annoyance in Johnny's face slipped over into curiosity. "What did the Navy do to you?"

Watson ignored that. "Do you know a lot about the Navy?"

Johnny looked sour, sure he had started a whole hour's conversation. "I know most anything," he said curtly, "from how to turn a battleship around to how to stand anchor watch." He glanced at Katie and saw her looking at him. "Come on, Katie—"

"I won't be long," Watson said, almost pleading, "but it's awfully important. Every time I meet a sailor I ask a question I've been trying to have answered for a long time."

"Couldn't any of them answer it?" Johnny said, retreating ever so slightly.

"They all give different answers," Watson said sadly.

"What's it got to do with the Navy ruining your life?" Johnny asked hotly.

"Once I was married," Watson said with deepest melancholy.

Johnny glanced sharply at Katie, and Katie knew what the glance meant: marriage seemed to be the only subject under discussion anywhere in New York City that morning.

"Julia, that was my wife," Watson continued, "was fifteen years older than me, but for the first few weeks it seemed like the perfect marriage although it's so long ago now that maybe I don't remember exactly right and may have made that up."

Katie looked at Johnny. In spite of his annoyed impatience his interest was being caught by something he had not encountered before.

"We lived in Hazleton, Pennsylvania—either of you come from there?—and I thought she was happy in Hazleton. Maybe nobody's really happy there. At any rate, she wanted to go to New York. She'd never been out of Hazleton. She bought New York newspapers, postcards, collected New York timetables—a regular magpie with a New York complex. And when I came home from a hard day at my store—I sold men's furnishings and the nicest line in Hazleton with special attention to outsizes—did she say, 'Have you had a hard day at the store?' She did not. She said, 'Aren't we ever going to get to New York?' "

Watson stopped, to finish his cigarette. "Do you find me monotonous?"

"Oh, no," Johnny said. "But I'm still waiting about the Navy."

"Finally I saved enough money to take Julia to New York." Watson looked inordinately proud. "We came here and we saw everything, the sky was the limit—Chinese restaurants, movies, sightseeing tours, and a Sunday on Staten Island. Then"—Watson lowered his voice—"on the fourteenth day, out of a clear cloudless sky, Julia ran away and left me, and I never saw her again. If she'd done it the first day, but to wait until I'd spent all my money—"

Johnny interrupted, "What's all that got to do with the Navy?"

"You will hear in a moment," Watson said solemnly. "She ran away with a sailor twenty years younger than she was. That's what the Navy did to me, and it's an aggravation."

Katie saw Johnny trying to hold back his laughter.

Watson shook his head. "Sailors always laugh. But what I want to know and what I'm always asking sailors is, what did a woman like that see in a sailor?"

"What do sailors say?"

"They all give different answers," Watson confessed sadly. "Some say she got restless, some say it was a mother instinct, some say she got a sort of sea fever."

"Maybe she was sick of Hazleton," Johnny suggested.

Watson shook his head. "There's something special about sailors and women."

Johnny took a bow for all navies, from the days of triremes to P-T boats. "That's what I've discovered."

"I've always wondered what it is," Watson admitted, "but no sailor can ever tell me."

Katie interrupted. "Maybe you ought to ask a woman."

"Yeah," Johnny said, his impatience suddenly full returned. "Well, that's that."

"But that's not all," Watson said. "Another thing perplexes me."

"What's that?"

Watson shook his head. "What did any sailor see in her? Tell me that! Maybe he saw something in her I didn't see myself and that thought has haunted me for twenty years."

Johnny had no answer for that. He turned again to Katie. "Come on, Katie—"

"I wonder if I could ask a favor—" Watson said timidly.

"Now what?"

"If you could spare, perhaps, a few dollars—"

Johnny reacted instantly. "Sure." He took out his wallet while Katie frowned. "I guess the Navy owes you a few dollars," he said, glad to pay anything to get rid of an annoyance.

"Thank you, sailor, thanks." Watson said, bowing. "I hope you'll be happy in your marriage."

Johnny's face clouded. "Listen, you—" But Watson was already heading down the path.

"You shouldn't have given him money—he probably gets it from all sailors," Katie said.

"Anything to get him to go," Johnny said bluntly. "All the time he was talking all I could think of was how we were wasting time. It's almost ten-thirty. Only about six hours left." He shook his head and sighed deeply. "I never saw a day go so fast."

"Neither did I." And she thought now life would be different.

He would be gone today, but she would have the hope that he might come back. That hope was like having a throb stir in something long inert.

"Katie!" Johnny made that sound a prayer, a hope, almost a call for help. He looked straight into her eyes, asking understanding, and hesitated no more. "I want to be alone with you somewhere, somewhere where we can be alone, see?"

Katie felt his hand tighten on hers while his words tightened her body. Her smile of amusement at the way Johnny had approached what she had long ago guessed could have been a smile of half-promised agreement or a smile of understanding at his obvious embarrassment. But she said carefully, "Is that the fifth thing you wanted to do ashore?"

Johnny held back an answer for a second, then said bluntly, "Yes."

"With any girl at all?"

"With any girl at all," he said truthfully, "until I saw you." Then he added hurriedly, hopefully, "And we have so little time left." Like a man anticipating sure argument he said, "Of course, it would be easier, I guess, if it were night and a moon and all that."

"Easier?"

"Easier to ask you. And maybe you'd understand better too."

"Don't you think I understand, Johnny?" Katie asked softly.

Johnny went on, floundering. "Here in broad daylight maybe it does sound funny."

"It's people who matter at times like this, not surroundings," Katie answered. "And I do understand and it doesn't sound funny. I love you. Why should it sound funny?"

Johnny was somewhat taken aback. "Well, I just thought, maybe—"

Katie swung around to him, her gray eyes steady, and said, "I'd like to be alone with you too, and now. And for a little while or forever." The frank sudden astonishment on his face made her laugh. "You look so surprised! Didn't I tell you I loved you?"

"Yes," Johnny said. Then, in deepest sincerity, "I love you, Katie."

For a few moments they sat silent, knowing no words to say, too filled with the glow of life and love to hunt words. Katie felt Johnny's arm around her shoulder, resting strong and warm on her.

Then Johnny said quietly, "Where can we go, Katie?"

"It doesn't matter. Where do sailors usually go?"

Johnny looked embarrassed. "To hotels, all kinds of hotels. But I don't know much about them in New York."

"I don't know any hotels or places like that," Katie answered. In her same simple matter-of-fact voice she continued, "The only place I can think of is my room way over in Brooklyn, but it's hot there and it isn't very nice."

"You just said it was the people that mattered, not the surroundings."

"I did that," Katie admitted. Then, suddenly, "Oh, Johnny, I wish you didn't have to go away, ever, ever!"

He did not answer. With one simple intent he added, "If we have to go all the way to Brooklyn, we'd better be going."

"It's pretty far," Katie agreed. She hung tight to his arm as they rose from the bench.

"Can we get a taxi?"

"It's hard to persuade a driver to go so far—maybe if we're lucky. But first we have to walk quite a way to get out of the Park."

Johnny groaned. "Why did we come in so far for?" Then he smiled. "The way I feel now though, I'd walk to either end of the world."

Katie squeezed his arm. "I feel the same way."

He turned to her, pulled her close to him and kissed her.

The pressure of his lips stayed with her. They walked on in the rising beat of their hearts. Now and then Katie glanced at Johnny to smile at him and found him smiling at her. Then, suddenly feeling out of breath, Katie noticed that they were walking faster and faster. She said, gasping, "Do we have to run?"

Johnny answered, "You said it was far, didn't you?"

They cut down a path behind the Zoo. An old Austrian couple saw them coming and smiled as they passed. The man said to the woman, "*Liebchen*, did you see their faces?"

His wife nodded. "Only on the faces of the very young or the very happy do you see that look."

From the path a broad strip of lawn led to a roadway, and, beyond that, to Fifth Avenue and taxis. As they crossed the lawn Katie said, "Johnny, I'm out of breath again."

For a second they stopped while Johnny lit a cigarette. He took a deep puff and said gently, "Come on, it's just a little way now. I can even see taxis on the street."

On the path near by a large awkward sailor came roll-ing along, the swing of the sea in his clumsy stride. His face was turned to the sun. It was a strong face, bumpy, and filled with assorted features. It was scarred on one cheek. A bulbous and bent nose shadowed a heavy mouth. His uniform fitted him as tightly as a balloon cover. His shoulders were so broad that he seemed about to pop out of his jumper. Its collar rode up and down with each step.

He happened to glance toward Johnny and Katie. His huge jaw dropped for a moment. He came forward on the double, holding to his hat and wobbling as he ran.

He called, "Hey, Johnny!"

Johnny turned as if spun round by concussion. His face lost its color. As Katie felt his hand shake suddenly she looked at him. More than color had drained from his face.

"Johnny!" the sailor said loudly. "Who's the dame?"

Johnny looked shriveled and seared.

"So you followed my advice, huh? I'm proud of you!" The sailor's broad smile turned to a scowl at getting no answer. "Say, aren't you going to introduce me? That's manners, my boy."

In a dead voice Johnny said, "This is Katie. Katie, this is one of my shipmates."

"Paul Lardlisky, seaman first class."

"Is this Lardlips?" Katie asked.

He frowned at Johnny, and when he frowned it was not a threat of dark cloud but a whole sky going black. "Not many call me that when I'm around in person."

"He's one of the men in my watch," Johnny explained futilely.

"The best sailor in the whole damn Navy too," Lard-lips added. "Eighteen years in it. If there's anything I don't know about it, the brass hats haven't thought it up yet."

Such sudden foreboding flickered in Johnny's face that Katie could not look at him for more than a second at a time. He avoided her glance and looked as if he wished he were forty feet under sea, without a ripple on the surface. Assurance, firmness, even the freshness in his face, all were gone.

"Well, well!" Lardlips stepped off a pace and looked Katie over from head to foot, stopping admiringly long enough at her full high breasts, at her waist, at her rightly carved ankles. "How'd you pick as shapely a doll as this Johnny, and so early in the morning? A regular destroyer! Looks as if she sails too."

Johnny seemed unable to find any words but his face showed what he felt, a complete and shaking premonition of what each additional second might bring.

"I looked all over for a doll but it was too early in the morning," Lardlips said with a broad tinge of sadness. "Usually you can find 'em at the hot-dog stand near the Central Park lake. All that's around there this morning is school kids in dirty socks who look like they'd spent the night under a rowboat."

Lardlips affected Katie like a strong whiff from a Sand Street cellar. She looked to Johnny for some clue to what next to do, but he stood rooted and undecided. Katie made her own decision quickly. She said, "If you'll excuse us, please, I'm pleased, indeed, to have made your acquaintance but we'll have to be going."

"Where in hell can you go this time of the morning?" Lardlips asked suspiciously.

"We got an engagement," Katie said breezily.

"Yeah," Johnny added weakly, "we had an engagement, sort of."

"Can't I come with you?"

"It's way over in Brooklyn," Katie said in a tone that would discourage an armadillo.

"I got nothing against Brooklyn," Lardlips insisted.

Katie looked at Johnny. He said, "Well, it wasn't very interesting. I don't think you'd like it."

"If it's not so important," Lardlips said with the tone of experience, "it won't matter if you skip it. Maybe we can eat lunch together and I'll tell you some of the stories I know." He shook his head vigorously. "I hate these goddam half-days ashore. I just can't get started. Come on, let's go somewhere." He took Johnny's arm and would have swung his arm around Katie's waist but she side-stepped it. "Jeez, I'm glad I found you. I get awful lonely when I'm alone."

Johnny smiled nervously at Katie.

She was confused at seeing him so upset and so thoroughly speechless.

"You see, Katie," Lardlips explained, taking a hold like a pipe wrench on her arm, "we kid Johnny a lot about dames. He doesn't know a damn thing about them, as I bet you've found out. But he's a good kid, even if he is only nineteen."

Katie understood at once Johnny's silence and a great deal more. She could not help glancing at him. So deep was his embarrassment that she was sorry to have looked. His neck, now deep red, was in sharp contrast to his blue collar.

"You couldn't find a better kid, if you like kids," Lardlips continued, "though a doll like you ought to prefer a man of real experience."

"Like you?" Johnny said, suddenly coming to life.

"Well," Lardlips said puffily, "if I wasn't so goddam modest I might say yes. But don't worry, kid, I won't steal her." He changed to a more intimate tone. "But I could go for you in a super way, baby. I could tell at a glance you're a sailor's girl. I remember once I was down in Trinidad, down in the Carrybeen. They got beautiful dolls too, Hindoo, Chinese, Negro, all mixed up. There was one little doll I saw, mostly Chinese. After a hell of a fight I took her away from a G.I., but I got awful smashed up because four guys jumped me at once. So the doll took me to her house to fix me up and damn if everything in the place hadn't come off American ships, sheets from the officers' quarters, tablecloths from their mess, even a blue smoking lamp." He laughed, half bray, half belch. "I just had a hunch when I saw that doll that she was a sailor's girl."

In spite of herself Katie exploded, "Oh, Johnny!" and

glanced aslant at him. He was looking off in the distance.
The color of his face now matched his neck.

Lardlips did not understand and looked suspicious.

"I heard that story," Katie said grimly.

"Johnny tell you? He's always telling stories about me!"
And Lardlips, after whanging him on the shoulder,
looked as proud as a new-made admiral sporting his first
public relations officer.

Katie did not look at Johnny now. She could imagine
how he felt. She hated the smug satisfaction on Lardlips'
face and wanted to run from him, but Johnny would have
to give the word. Yet, in a way, she was grateful to Lardlips for brushing away, at one monstrous sweep, much she
had not understood about Johnny.

"Come on, let's go," Lardlips said impatiently when
he saw Johnny standing still. "We can walk around, then
get something to eat. Maybe we can even find a place
with a floor show at noon. You never saw a floor show, I
bet, Johnny."

Katie saw Johnny trying to make up his mind, trying
to get the strength for any decision.

"If you're still afraid I'll take your doll," Lardlips repeated, noticing Johnny's hesitation, "forget it. I
wouldn't do that to a shipmate and, besides, I ain't got
time enough today."

"Or any other day," Katie snapped.

Lardlips shrugged his shoulders. "You serious about
this kid?" When he got no answer he looked worried,
and the wrinkles on his large face were deep-shadowed
troughs. "Say, he hasn't asked you to marry him, has he?"

That shattered Johnny's silence. "What the hell are you
talking about? Why the hell don't you mind your business
and beat it?"

"Me?" Lardlips looked shocked. "Beat it? Is that any
way to talk to the guy who weaned you on salt water?" He
turned again to Katie. "You don't look like the marrying
kind, so if what I said insulted you, I'm sorry. Of course,
now and then even a sailor gets fooled. Once I knew a doll
in Norfolk who was nuts about me and was always talk-

ing about a home and kids and damn near talked me into the idea." Then he told the story that Johnny had told about himself a few hours earlier. "Yes, sir," he concluded, "I sent half the fleet to knock at her door and ask for Nellie!" He laughed until he shook like a pot of coffee on a destroyer.

Katie annoyed at not knowing quite what to answer, said, "I heard that story before, from another sailor."

"The hell you say!" Lardlips was tickled. "I didn't think I was as well known in the Navy as that." He grinned at Johnny. "That's how you get famous, shipmate!" Then, with a nod like the swing of a bowsprit, he said, "It's dolls like that one in Norfolk the chaplain means when he talks about 'the perils of the sea.' In fact, as I tell Johnny and all the other young squirts many times, he means all marrying dolls." Then he swung around to Katie. "It's just as much for the doll's good. From marrying sailors, all dolls get is broken hearts."

Katie snorted. "From certain kinds of sailors, maybe."

Lardlips ignored that. "All Johnny knows about dolls I taught him, and the first lesson's a cinch: if you want something from a doll, don't beat the bushes, ask her right out for it. Maybe that ain't manners, but you'd be surprised how often it works."

By now Katie was ready to haul off and hit this large rubbery mass of self-confidence, but because Johnny would do nothing for himself she knew she could do nothing.

They were walking aimlessly. Lardlips was in control and Johnny was just being dragged along. And not far away, Katie saw, were Fifth Avenue and taxis going everywhere, perhaps even to Brooklyn.

From his store of experience Lardlips brought out one tale after another of the women he had known. "Eighteen years in the Navy," he said, "and no dame's hooked me yet. That's why they call me an able-bodied seaman!"

"That only proves that some women have luck," Katie said.

Lardlips ignored that. "Kids like Johnny always come

to me for advice. They're fresh from the farm, just like raw meat. You got to pickle and cure them in salt water. Eventually you make decent sailors out of them, but it's hard work for men like me. Now, take Johnny! Just a little while ago he was in South Dakota. He's still got chicken litter in his hair but give me time—"

"I think he's a good sailor already." Katie felt she had to defend Johnny. The complete humiliation she saw on his face was more than she could stand. Her earlier deep annoyance at him changed now to an even deeper desire to help him.. "He's a good sailor," she repeated firmly. "He's got that ribbon for bravery, hasn't he?"

Katie was wrong. She had not yet seen complete humiliation on his face. She saw it now as she looked proudly at Johnny.

"He has?" Lardlips asked. "That ribbon? Oh, sure. What did he tell you he got it for?"

Katie knew that she had made some mistake but she had to go through with it. "For diving off a ship and saving some officer."

Lardlips laughed until he got hiccups. "I'll say he's a good sailor. Kids the dolls on like a chief petty officer." He pounded Johnny a broadside of a wallop on the back while Kate felt increasingly confused. "Sure, he got that ribbon for lifesaving, but just the same I'll bet you he got it through his swimming test at boot camp being dragged on a rope."

"What is the ribbon?" Katie asked, not daring to ask Johnny.

"It's a special one," Lardlips said, still laughing uproariously. "They give it to Johnny for lifesaving but other soldiers and sailors get it for being in Europe or even just near it. There must be a whole factory somewhere making nothing but those ribbons." His fat stomach was still rolling like a ship's wake. "Wait till I tell that back on the ship!" His laughter slowly settled down. "Lifesaving!"

With her eyes flashing and her face reddened, Katie swung around to him. "Johnny and I have to go now," she said. She had to get Johnny alone, if only to apologize for having humiliated him through her own stupidity.

"Where are you going?" Lardlips asked bluntly.

"I was going to take Johnny to meet my kid brother," Katie said blandly. "He wants to hear about the Navy. He might join."

"Good, let's go."

"My family's only expecting me and Johnny for lunch."

"I'll go easy on the food," Lardlips said generously. "Besides, I can·do your brother good. I'm the best walking ad for the Navy there is."

Katie looked helplessly to Johnny but his face held no hope.

"Well, let's go." When he got no answer, Lardlips saw Johnny and Katie hesitating. A muddy cloud of suspicion settled on his face. "Say, what the hell's going on? You wouldn't be trying to dump me, would you?"

Just then a pleasant breeze flitted across the park. It lifted the blankets from babies sleeping in their carriages. It blew candy wrappers from the grass and rustled newspapers in the bushes. It twirled dust along the near-by road. And it flicked Lardlips' cap from his head, sailing it through the air. It fell a little way off.

"Damn!" he exploded. He went after the cap, ambling with the motion of an airborne whale.

His eyes plowing the grass, Johnny fumbled in his jumper pocket for a cigarette, then looked at Katie and tried to smile. The smile flickered out as he felt Katie's hand reach for his, and astonishment settled on his face. The cigarette waggled on his lips.

He said desperately, "My God, I wish he'd go and leave us alone."

"So do I," Katie spoke fervently.

Johnny stared at her with deepening surprise. "Do you really?"

"Let's run and grab a cab quick, anywhere, before he gets back."

Johnny shook his head. "He'd make things awful tough for me on shipboard and, believe me, he can."

Lardlips was coming back, his cap retrieved. He was brushing it carefully against his sleeve as if it were made of velvet and feathers. On his face was a curious, strained, noncomprehending look. He said awkwardly, "Well, Johnny!" He shook his head, trying to dislodge some unpleasant idea that would not go. "Well, I guess I better be going, Johnny."

Johnny's jaw dropped. He stared at Katie.

"Sure," Lardlips said, as if he did not quite believe himself, "why should I try to horn in on you kids? Go along to that phony date of yours, but God help you, Johnny, if you're a second late reporting back to the ship." He smiled at Katie. "You're quite a doll. Be good to the kid."

With that Lardlips waddled across the lawn into the Park.

"Well, I'll be damned," Johnny said, not quite believing what he saw. Then, when he realized that he was alone again with Katie, he looked around, as if hunting some exit. He had to say something and he could find nothing to say. He looked down to the ground, searching for something, and said, "Well, I guess I'll be going too."

"Where to?"

He shrugged his shoulders. "Back to the subway, I guess, then to the Navy Yard." He added in a limping voice, "I'd better not be late."

Katie smiled and wanted to throw her arms around his neck.

"You're such a little boy, Johnny!"

He bristled at once. "You wouldn't know anything about how old I am if it hadn't been for Lardlips!"

"If it hadn't been for him, I wouldn't really have known you."

He started to be angry at that, then said futilely, "You must think I'm a complete phony."

"No, I don't." Katie looked into his face and met his glance. "I don't, honest, I don't."

His glance wavered and dropped earthward.

"Johnny," Katie's voice was as soft as a wavelet against

an anchored ship, "don't you still want to go where we were going?"

Johnny straightened up like a man who had long been stooping in some dark hold and was now in the light. "You mean it?"

"Come on," Katie said, holding out her hand. "We're still wasting an awful lot of time."

Breathlessly they reached Fifth Avenue. Johnny stopped a cab and said, "We want to go to Brooklyn."

"York Street," Katie added hurriedly.

The driver shook his head. "Can't make that trip in wartime, lady."

"It's an emergency," Johnny said. "Come on, have a heart."

Katie tried her best smile. "It's really an emergency."

The driver hesitated for just a second. "Okeh, sailor, get in."

"If you know any short cuts, take them," Johnny said, slamming the door.

As they went down Fifth Avenue, with Johnny sitting close to her, his arm around her, he talked slowly and haltingly, stammering after full honesty. "I just don't understand women, I guess," he confessed. "That was why I hated Lardlips so. On shipboard he's always talking about his women and he knows a hell of a lot about them because he knows a hell of a lot of women."

"You don't need to know a lot of women to know a lot about them," Katie said. "One's plenty."

"I always thought women didn't like phonies."

"Did Lardlips tell you that? He doesn't know anything about some kinds of women. Johnny, would you think I was a phony if I told you I was eighteen instead of twenty?" She waited to see the slight surprise on his face. "Well, I am."

Johnny did not answer that directly. He said, "Lardlips was always bragging about his women and about how much money he spends on them—" he began to stammer —"and—and—"

"Hush, Johnny," Katie said, kissing him.

The taxi jolted to a stop to avoid a bus and threw them apart.

"I made a bet with him I'd find a girl before nine a.m.," Johnny continued, "and I did! And I wanted the time on the picture to prove it."

"And I'm glad you found me, so glad!"

Katie put her head on his shoulder. They rode on in silence. For the closeness Katie was grateful; the closeness was alive and vibrant, and she felt it through all her body. Johnny seemed to sink deep in his own thoughts as if all that had happened in the last half hour had numbed him.

After a long silence Johnny said, "That was funny how Lardlips went away so suddenly."

"Maybe there's a charm over us," Katie said.

"Sure there is. That's what brought us together this morning."

Katie shook her head. "We both wished Lardlips would go and he went."

"Nothing to do with it," Johnny answered promptly. "He is a pretty decent guy. He finally caught on that he wasn't wanted and beat it."

Katie was not so sure. "Remember that white duck? We both wished he'd come and he came."

Johnny laughed. "That proves you're wrong. A duck is so stubborn not even a charm could make him do anything he didn't want to do."

"Anyway," Katie agreed, "we've had everything we've wished for today and now I have what I want most."

"What's that?"

"You." Katie turned to him and kissed him. He returned her kiss absently, then with slow tightening, as some voltage deep within him was increased, and he held her so close she had to break for breath.

He glanced out of the window. "It's a long way to Brooklyn, isn't it?"

"It's always long to Brooklyn when you want to get there fast."

Johnny asked, "What kind of a place do you live in?"

"Not much. You'll see." Then Katie felt concerned. She hoped she had left her room neat but she could not remember; that seemed so long ago. And she was concerned too about something else. "I hope Mrs. Healy, that's my landlady, isn't home. I don't know what I'll say to her if we meet her."

"Tell her I'm a long-lost brother just back from seven years at sea." Johnny had recovered a little of his earlier gaiety.

"I never took anyone to my room—you know—" Katie said awkwardly. "Maybe Mrs. Healy'll be out at a store at this time of the morning."

"Sure, everything'll be all right," Johnny said carelessly. "We've been lucky all day. You said so."

The cab crossed Manhattan Bridge, turned through a tangle of crowded streets, then came to an old house with a stoop and a rusty iron railing. Katie said, with no pride, "Here we are."

For what seemed like the first time she noticed how dirty and unswept the street was, how ramshackle the house looked with its railings loose in its concrete base, with paint peeling on the door, and the latch broken and rusty. The gilding on the sign "Furnished Rooms" was spotty and faded. She had never really noticed these things before and wondered why she should see them so clearly now and feel embarrassed. But if Johnny saw anything that displeased him he did not show it.

As Katie led the way into the vestibule she felt her heart begin to pound. The hallway was quiet and empty. The usual collection of rusty baby carriages was gone. From the basement below came the odor of meat loaf baking, heavy with onions. Katie felt anew the whole greasy air of the world around and wished she were leading Johnny into one of those apartments on high rooftops which the movies always showed, with sun and air and green things. But she forgot that as she headed for the stairs with Johnny close behind. The first door to be passed was Mrs. Healy's, and, as Mrs. Healy was fond of saying, she ran a respectable house.

With no sound but their own soft footsteps and the squeak of one stairboard after another, they went up the first two flights.

At the second landing Katie saw the trash box, an unsightly mess, ringed by unwashed milk bottles and paper bundles of floor sweepings.

Then, somewhere downstairs, a door opened, and a moment later there was a first heavy tread on the staircase.

"How far?"

"Two flights more."

"It's like going topside from the engine room."

Katie tried to walk even more quietly but almost every stairboard on the last flight squeaked. But it was not loud enough to drown out the slow heavy steps coming piston-like from the first flight below.

At the fourth landing Katie hurried to the rear door, unlocked it, and almost pulled Johnny into the room. She locked the door and whispered, "I won't know what to say to her."

"What will she do?"

"She'll be storming mad."

"I'm not afraid of landladies," Johnny said gallantly.

"She'll make you go."

"Hhm!" Johnny said. "We'll see."

The steps were turning the second landing now.

"Even if she does throw us out I'm going to kiss you once." Johnny came to Katie. His hat fell off in his hurry.

"Hush, not yet." Katie felt every nerve pulled tight as the steps turned the third-floor landing. "Oh, I wish she'd go away."

"So do I," Johnny said. "Boy, so do I!"

The steps hesitated for a second and there was silence in the hallway. Then they sounded again on the stairs but this time they were going down.

"See!" Katie said triumphantly.

"See what?"

"We're under some kind of charm. We both wished she would go and she did."

Johnny laughed. "I think I heard the doorbell ring. Or maybe she remembered something on the stove."

Katie listened for another moment. The steps were far fainter now. Her face showed her relief. "Well, she is gone, and glory be to God!"

"Yeah!" Johnny agreed. He seemed suddenly ill at ease as he looked around the small room. "It's a little place, isn't it?"

"Awful little." Katie went over and opened the window.

The room was just large enough to hold a single bed against one wall, a small table, a broad dresser, and one chair.

"But it's nice," Johnny said, as if it were vital to keep going the most impersonal conversation possible.

With a trace of a smile Katie agreed, "It is nice."

Johnny walked to the dresser, brushing close to Katie as he passed. There was a long row of photographs against the mirror. He suddenly became awfully interested in them. "You got a lot of pictures."

Katie came close to him and explained them. There was one of her sister and a couple of children, picnic pictures of some of the Lushman employees, a postcard from Yellowstone Park, and a card with an Irish shamrock on it. Largest of all was an autographed picture of Barry Fitzgerald.

"Who's the man?" Johnny asked.

"A movie actor."

"You know him?"

Katie laughed. "Of course not. You send a letter to Hollywood asking for a picture and you get it. He's Irish."

"Oh," Johnny said as if relieved and as if it were something to be relieved over. "A lot of sailors have pictures like that of Hollywood girls. Some of them are pretty good-looking, really good-looking," he repeated, eager to keep the conversation going. "And they have beautiful faces."

Katie, close beside him, nodded.

Then, impetuously, Johnny swung to her and put his arms around her and held her tight. She fitted herself shamelessly against him, almost impatiently, feeling the warm promise of his fresh young body through her thin dress.

"Oh, Johnny," she managed to whisper, "I love you so much."

He said nothing but went awkwardly after her lips. From his timid awkwardness, his rough eagerness, Katie was sure of something else about Johnny, something that raised and strengthened the singing within her.

"Oh, Johnny, Johnny," she said with new happiness. "Wait a minute. We have all day."

"Honest?"

"Until the last minute before you have to run," Katie said. She was out of breath for the moment.

Johnny smiled at her, then lit a cigarette. He looked for a place to sit down. He carefully avoided the bed and sat on the one chair. "Those Hollywood girls, you know," he said thoughtfully, "none of them have hair and eyes like yours."

Katie could feel her whole body vibrate. "I just wish we weren't here just one day. I wish this was just the first day of a lot of days." She continued dreamily, while Johnny puffed on his cigarette, "I wish I'd be waiting for you every time you come ashore in our own little apartment. If we were married—"

Johnny looked up sharply. "We couldn't get married today even if we wanted to."

"Sure we could," Katie contradicted gaily. "Don't you remember Hosenfenster?"

Johnny stood up, alarmed.

"You mean it, right now?"

His tone surprised Katie. She said frankly, "Yes, of course, if you want to."

"You mean you could stop—right here, now, and go off?"

"More than anything in the world," Katie said, without the faintest idea of what Johnny was driving at.

Johnny's face hardened. He looked puzzled and disappointed. "That's what Lardlips said."

"Lardlips?" Katie had never expected to hear that name again.

"He was always talking about dames who take you off to their places," he said most distrustfully, "and get you in a weak moment and then before you know it you promise things and get a hawser tossed over you for life."

Katie's hands slipped to her hips. She turned slowly and faced him. "Do you honestly think that describes me?"

"Lardlips—"

"I should think you'd have enough of his smartness to last you for life." Katie was so furious that nothing else mattered for the moment but the heat of her anger. "How can you say a thing like that after what happened in the Park?"

Johnny said defiantly, "I'm not ashamed of anything that happened."

"There's no reason for you to be," Katie answered. She shook her head slowly. "Oh, Johnny!"

He shook his head, not understanding. "After Lardlips made a fool out of me, you could have walked off. I don't see why you didn't. I would have. Most dames I ever heard of would have."

"Why didn't I?"

"I don't know," he said uneasily.

Katie's lip curled. "Because I had my heart so set on marrying you?"

"I don't know," Johnny answered helplessly.

"You're such a baby, Johnny. You don't know anything about women or being in love. Look, Johnny, I'll tell you something a lot of men don't know or don't remember. A woman likes to be with a man. There!" She looked into his puzzled face. "Sometimes a woman wants a man even more than any lonely sailor wants a woman, and feels just as bad too. But it's got to be the right man."

The look on Johnny's face was indescribable.

"You looked shocked or something, Johnny. But that's the way I feel about you." Before she could think of the consequences, she added, "I'm sure you've never been with a woman before, like this."

He blushed, and his anger at once equaled hers. "Maybe so, maybe not. But I didn't come for a lecture about myself."

Katie was too surprised to say more than, "Oh, Johnny!"

"I don't need any woman in my life," he added defiantly. "Permanently, that is. There's nothing in this world any woman can do for me. Nothing!"

That hurt and deeply but Katie knew the best answer was softness. "Some day you might be surprised," she said quietly. "That's another thing you find out when you grow up. Sometimes a woman can do a lot for a man."

"What?" Johnny snapped.

She shook her head and stepped back. Her hands were awkwardly at her side. Johnny was just a few feet off, in the narrowness of that little room, but at that moment he might have been a thousand miles at sea. They faced each other, with no words left to say. Then, on impulse, she threw herself on Johnny. "Oh, you baby, you don't even know when a woman loves you, just for you, not for anything else in the world."

"I guess I don't," Johnny admitted awkwardly, trying to smooth her hair with a large rough hand. "I guess I don't." Then he looked down on her face with surprise. "What are you crying for?"

"I'm not crying much," Katie insisted, "and I'll stop. I guess it's because of the way we're wasting time and never will it come back to us."

"Uh huh," Johnny said. "I guess so." He fumbled after his cigarettes and lit another one.

Katie went to the dresser and got out a handkerchief.

"It's funny," Johnny said, half amused, "but Lardlips said that too."

"What did he say?" Katie swung around, the handkerchief at her eyes.

"He said you meet many dames who try everything and when nothing works they turn on the tears."

"Johnny!" Katie's face and voice flared red again. "Why do you keep bringing Lardlips up all the time?"

"I don't mean that the way it sounded, honest I didn't," Johnny answered. "I just think of those things, that's all."

"Well, let's forget him," Katie said curtly. "You're old enough to stand on your own feet without any help from him."

"There's another thing," Johnny said as if he were being driven to it, "you keep repeating how young I am and how I don't know anything about women. Well, Lardlips said that was another one—they try to mother you. You might think I needed a mother."

"And even try to get allotments the way that Hosie said?"

Johnny did not answer.

"You're so full of fears, Johnny," Katie said slowly, "maybe it would have been better if we hadn't come here. I didn't think you'd be so scared and suspicious."

"Who's scared and of what?" Johnny asked, his voice harsh and brittle. "I just didn't expect to get talked to, that's all."

Katie walked to the window and turned her back. Here, she was sure, was a situation she did not know how to handle, one that made her feel completely helpless. She said thoughtfully, "When you say things like that I wish you weren't here."

"So do I," Johnny said nervously. "So do I."

She stood at the window, looking down on a dirty and littered back yard. She was baffled at Johnny's angry replies. Probably embarrassment and fear and real uncertainty all contributed to them, and a sense of some inadequacy. Perhaps she was to blame. "Let's forget, Johnny, and start over," she said, turning around.

Then she blinked and only with force held back a scream.

Johnny was gone, as completely as if he had never been there. Thinking it might be a game, she wasted seconds looking wildly around the room, even looking under the bed, seeing everything with such sudden tears that even familiar things looked strange. Then she hurried to the door, stumbling in her haste to get it open.

Far below she heard quick descending steps. She would have screamed his name but for fear of Mrs. Healy. Instead, she went back to her room, grabbed her purse, and hurried down the steps and into the street. There was no sign of Johnny. A huckster was selling fruit from an open wagon; some children were playing ball; and one lone old man was coming along carrying a huge bundle.

For a moment she stood daubing at her eyes, concerned only with the problem of how to find Johnny again, how to find him and tell him that nothing ever mattered so long as he knew she loved him, that no fear need ever separate them again. She stood hesitantly in the full sun on the grimy street before deciding what to do. In a moment she knew.

"Oh, Johnny, Johnny," she whispered as she hurried along the sidewalk, prepared to follow him to the dimmest and farthest ends of a shadowed earth, if there she might find him.

*   *   *

The noon sun hung like a broiler flame over the Sands Street gate at the Navy Yard. There Katie waited through that long hot day. Although there were other gates to the Yard she knew that almost all sailors used this entrance. She waited with assurance; he had to be back at five. Before five he would come along.

In a thin blue and white stream sailors passed in and out through the gate. Gray trolleys ground and screeched their way along the bumpy Sands Street tracks. For Katie everything was blurry and out of focus so long as the face she waited for did not appear. While she waited and the hot sun streaked her face and her clothes she kept repeating, "Just once, God in heaven, just once. I don't even know where to write him and he'll never find me again."

As the afternoon passed slowly Katie kept telling herself that Johnny had to come along, that the next sailor or the next or the next to come in sight would be

Johnny. She could imagine the joy of seeing him, even if he came at the next to the last minute, the joy of throwing her arms around him and telling him that no matter what he said, no matter what he thought, she loved him more than the world and all that was in it.

She waited first on one corner, then the other, turning down a dozen invitations from hopeful sailors. Watching the long narrow street, she wondered idly about the haste of his departure. Then she remembered that almost the last thing she had said was, "I wish you weren't here." And Johnny had answered, "So do I." So often that day she had said, "There's a charm over us. What we wish for we get." Any charm was a cruel charm that took Johnny away. The whole thought of a charm was nonsense; Johnny had left when fear and embarrassment and complete lack of assurance overpowered every other desire. Softly she said, "If all we have to do to make a thing happen is to wish it, then I wish Johnny were back, right now, right here, with me."

The screech of a trolley was the only answer.

As the afternoon came toward its end, the hot sun brought up an earth mist and changed the blue of the sky to sultry gray. It was past four.

For the first time Katie faced the chance that Johnny might not come by, that he might have gone through another gate, that he was already on his ship. Her eyes burned from tears held back and her throat felt rake-scraped. She thought of running now to other gates, of doing anything that would take away the hopelessness of doing nothing but waiting.

She crossed over nervously to the Marine guards at the turnstiles by the gate. "How do I get a pass into the Yard?" she asked.

"Ask in the office here. Why do you want a pass?"

Katie hesitated, hoping she would not be laughed at. "I want to find a sailor."

The laughter that followed hit Katie like a fist.

"If we gave passes for that, we'd have so many dames in here we couldn't get the ships out!" the marine roared.

Katie held back tears and asked in a voice as steady as she could hold it, "Do you know a sailor named Johnny Smith?"

"What's that? What did you say the name was?"

"Johnny Smith."

The marine grinned and called to another guard, "Dame here wants to know if we know a sailor named Johnny Smith."

"Are you kidding?" the marine grunted. "Ask her if he spells it with a 'y.' "

The first marine was still laughing. "What color sailor suit was he wearing?"

Katie turned away. It was past four-thirty. For the next few minutes she stood counting the time. It went fast. Once or twice she thought she saw him coming but each time the tall lithe sailor walking so airily to the gate turned out to be a stranger. Then she felt that perhaps some of the sailors now hurrying down the street might be on Johnny's ship. She stopped one, a studious-looking redhead. "Do you know a Johnny Smith on your ship?"

"Can't give out information like that, sister," he said. "Write to the Secretary of the Navy. But if you'd like to give me your telephone number I'll speak to him myself."

Some of these men, she was sure, would see Johnny this night, would have dinner with him, would see him sit thoughtfully on the edge of his bunk, thinking, frowning, wondering over the day ashore.

Somewhere a whistle blew, then another one. It was five o'clock and Katie had to reach to a lamp post to steady herself for a second.

Afternoon rusted to twilight and twilight faded to dark and the night came down, but she did not move from the corner, although she knew it was useless to wait any longer. River whistles were a blatant reminder that between her and Johnny, now and forever, there would be only miles of water never to be bridged, never crossed.

She turned up Sands Street, walking slowly and aimlessly. She passed the place where the morning had begun. She remembered that on this very same street in the early morning she had anticipated a lonely night, but certainly not one such as this, with its sterile bitterness and empty mystery. It would be impossible for her to return to her room. Johnny would be too much in it, and forever, standing there beside the dresser, sitting awkwardly on the chair.

She went on, lost in her mind and lost in the world, reviewing each second of the short day. She thought of the Coffee Pot and the subway ride and then the Waldorf. And Mrs. O'Geoghan! She was the one person in the world to whom she could talk about Johnny, and she did not live far away. With a definite objective Katie began to walk rapidly and found her way to High Street. Here Mrs. O'Geoghan lived on the top floor of an old house, in a little two-room apartment kept as spotless as any hotel suite.

Mrs. O'Geoghan came to the door in a bright cotton wrapper. Her stringy hair was curled tight in papers. She smiled broadly when she saw Katie. "I never thought you'd be coming, and least of all tonight," she said. "And if I had a young man the likes of him this morning—" She looked more closely at Katie's face and said gently, "Poor Katie, come in, my dear."

She put her arm around Katie's shoulder and drew her into the room.

"Sit down, Katie," she said with infinite gentleness. "You needn't say a word. I can guess."

A kettle was boiling on a little stove. Mrs. O'Geoghan went to it, matching the speed of her words to the kettle's hum. "I was just sitting down to hot tea, me lacking the strength in my legs to run after a bottle of beer. Tea'll be good for us. It's comforted many a girl when her man's gone away, and you aren't the first and won't be the last."

"Thank you," Katie said, feeling a little stronger from the mere touch of friendliness.

"Not a word until you've warmed yourself with tea." Mrs. O'Geoghan looked at her approvingly. "And even when you've warmed yourself, you need be telling me little I couldn't guess."

Katie obeyed gladly, drinking her tea in silence, while Mrs. O'Geoghan hovered over her.

"Sure, and I can tell you what you're going to say, Katie dear," Mrs. O'Geoghan continued. "You're going to tell me the young man who was with you this morning is gone, without so much as thanks, leaving you only desolation."

Katie nodded and forced herself to hold back her tears while she sipped her tea.

"The likes of men," Mrs. O'Geoghan said piously. "They're all like the long-legged Callahan goat at Ballinasloe my mother never could catch, always running— after he got what he wasn't supposed to have."

Katie shook her head.

"Johnny went away before that."

Mrs. O'Geoghan looked astonished. "Now, there is something new under the broad sun." She shook her head sadly. "And perhaps for a woman that's worse, but I wouldn't know that. No men ever left me like that, the conniving scoundrels."

Katie finished her tea and put the cup down. "I'm grateful to you," she said. "I feel better." Then, quietly and frankly, she told the story of the day. Mrs. O'Geoghan sat opposite, following the tale as she would have followed a love story in the movies, clucking, nodding, and wiping her eyes on her sleeve as Katie finished. And Katie left nothing out, nothing of her own feelings. "So many things hurt," she said, summing it up, "but most of all when he said, 'There's nothing no woman can ever do for me, ever.' "

Mrs. O'Geoghan agreed, adding, "He knows where you work. Some day he'll be coming there to find you."

Katie shook her head firmly. "He'll not seek me out again."

"He must have been nervous to go so fast," Mrs. O'Geoghan said, "and so quietly. The likes of such grass fever I never heard."

"I frightened him away," Katie said, "and that will burden me always. If I were only able to find him and tell him!"

A faint flush of hope lit Mrs. O'Geoghan's face. "Perhaps if I write to my sons, Dennis, Patrick, Michael, Francis, or Liffey—especially Liffey. He gets around a lot and never was one for staying in his own garden, house, or bed, in that respect being just like his father, and I doubt the Navy could change him much. Perhaps they may find your Johnny."

"How can anyone find a sailor named Johnny Smith?" Katie asked hopelessly. "There must be a million of them." She folded her arms on the table and rested her head. "I drove him away myself just by talking too much."

"It was funny, his going like that," Mrs. O'Geoghan agreed. "He didn't give you his home address or anything like that or any other clue to find him out?"

Katie shook her head. Then she sat up listlessly. "All I have is a photograph of him with me"—she reached in her handbag—"and this." She took out Johnny's souvenir medal from Belfast.

"Hhm, that's not much of a clue," Mrs. O'Geoghan said, looking at the coin with no great interest. Then something she saw startled her and she began to examine it very closely. "My eyes wouldn't lie over what I have in my fingers but I cannot believe it."

"What?"

"Have you never heard, Katie, of the coin of O'Flaherty?"

Katie shook her head.

"I've heard my grandmother describe this a hundred times," she said reverently. "Did you not say you both wished you weren't in the room?"

"Yes," Katie said hesitantly.

"And many times the day long you both wished for something and it happened?"

"Yes," Katie admitted.

Mrs. O'Geoghan held the coin high. "Here! This explains it—why he left so suddenly, why the Lard party left! You had this in your possession and you both wished it. As simple as that!"

Katie looked at her with plain disbelief. "Everything that happened as we wished could have had plain and natural causes."

"With so many things you wished, happening just so?" Mrs. O'Geoghan waved a fine skeptical hand.

"But what you are saying is impossible."

"Believe as you wish, Katie, but for meself, with so many things happening just so, it's too much for my mind to believe in what you call plain and natural causes. What I say makes much more simple sense." Mrs. O'Geoghan held the coin carefully in her hand. "My grandmother used to tell it and I've heard it from her many times. In Oughterard, in County Galway where she lived, Paddy White was a sheepherder. Suddenly he became the richest man in the west of Ireland. Was that plain and natural cause? Everybody knew he had found an O'Flaherty coin in his pasture. Four of them were made by Colm O'Flaherty more than a thousand years ago, in the days when men still knew how to make such things. In those days the O'Flahertys ruled the western shores and kept them free. And it was always said Colm O'Flaherty made the coins because he was weary of hearing his people say daily, till his eardrums were beat like the rocks off Aran, 'The Irish are a cursed and unlucky folk.' "

She looked tenderly at the coin. "The Irish who hold these, my grandmother used to say, will always be lucky and all their wishes granted, can they but find someone they love who wants the same thing honestly with them. Since the Irish live in prideful loneliness, such a person is not always easy for an Irishman to find. Sometimes you'd be searching the world over, in lonesome places, and in all the high mountains on the earth and tall ships on the seas before you'd find another Irishman to agree to want the same thing as another Irishman." Mrs. O'Geoghan chuckled to herself. "My grandmother used to say that Colm O'Flaherty made it that way on purpose, not wanting to have things too easy for the Irish and be spoiling them."

Katie smiled and shook her head. "There are no such miracles today."

Mrs. O'Geoghan bristled angrily. "Katie Morrison, from Connemara, and you saying that? The Irish can always believe easily in miracles—without them how would there be an Ireland? It's the simple everyday facts of life we find beyond understanding." She looked at Katie and laughed. "And it's not becoming to you to look so doubtful. What I'm telling you is true. That's the ever-green glory of the Irish—their stories are always true. It's only in the telling or writing of them that splendid imaginations overpower them." Then, with gentler voice, she continued, "When I was a little girl we would hunt in meadows and by the edges of the hills for an O'Flaherty coin because my grandmother said if we looked sharp we might find one." She added reminiscently, "Maybe she was just trying to get us out of the house. All I ever found for my seeking was an old half crown with some bloody Englishman's head on it and a counterfeit one at that. You never could trust the English."

Kate just listened, not knowing what to think, but steadily remembering tales like these and tones like those heard in childhood and then believed as easily as the peat fire on the hearth, the low white mist rising from the bogs, or the restless wind at the shutters were believed. And right here and now, she admitted, was a miracle; here and now in Brooklyn, neither the tales of childhood nor the tones nor the peat smoke, fog, fire, nor the wind nor the rattle of the shutters seemed very far away.

"And my grandmother, God rest her weary soul, used to say another thing," Mrs. O'Geoghan recalled softly. "He who possessed a coin, she said, was blessed with another power. He could, if he wished it as he lay down at the end of a day, roam the broad world by night while asleep looking for someone he loved, with never a guarantee that he'd find what he sought. That was what my grandmother used to call the luck of the Irish—always set with banns and limits and never guaranteed."

Katie, listening closely, did not move, but some of the restlessness and sorrow was gone from her face.

"And even that searching was beset with grave dangers," Mrs. O'Geoghan said, "for sometimes those who searched to no avail might never quite return to themselves. My grandmother always told about Paddy White's brother, Thomas, him who stole the coin from him and killing his own brother to do it. Always thereafter he was telling tales of the wonders of strange lands, who never once left his homeland and the steep stony streets of Ballyvaghan. But a day came when Thomas was judged apart forever from his daily life, and his friends put him in the crazy house at Galway, and he kept raving with a madness about searching and searching and never an end to it."

Very carefully Katie reached out and took the coin from Mrs. O'Geoghan's hand. Katie's quick movement as she stood up frightened the woman. She looked into Katie's face and what she saw frightened her the more. "Katie!"

"I must be going, Mrs. O'Geoghan."

"Going to where?"

"Home."

"Wait a little and take more tea," Mrs. O'Geoghan protested, a streak of fright in her voice. "Has anything I've been telling you upset you?"

"Upset me?" Katie smiled. "No, honestly no." Very carefully she put the coin back in her purse and as carefully put her purse under her arm.

"Will you come back soon, Katie?" Mrs. O'Geoghan sounded anxious, like one trying to delay even for a moment a traveler about to leave forever for the ends of the earth. She went on rapidly, "My son, Liffey, the unmarried one, will be home on leave next week. He'll have little to recommend himself to you as a husband but he's tall and proud to look on and he does have his father's coal-black eyes. And I can recommend meself as a mother-in-law." She stopped, with the click of a sob, sure that Katie was not listening to a word she said.

"I'll come back sometime," Katie promised gently. "And now, good night."

She went down the stairs and into the humid street, her head high, and all that was fresh and young in the swing of her moving body. Passers-by sometimes turned to look at her, caught by the way the night lights plated her pale blond hair with gold. Some of them noticed her eyes too, not their color, but the living flame in them, like the heat and light seen through the little peering window of the flaming boilers of a pounding ship.

2.

*O*F THE SEAMEN WHO SAW HER AND
of what then happened there are many tales.

.The chief petty officer on the *Dewey* saw her one night
and gave chase down a companionway but lost her. Knowing that Australian wives were trying to smuggle themselves to America, he had the ship searched for the next
three days. A lieutenant, U.S.N., on the *Myron* saw her
and thereby started a row in the wardroom. He accused
another lieutenant, U.S.N.R., who was always boasting
about his luck with women, of bringing her aboard. That
one went to the bridge for final settlement and apologies.

A quartermaster caught sight of her on the stern of the
Pasadena and could not sleep for nights. He had fathered
a child with a girl in San Francisco, then run. The woman
died. He was sure her ghost was following him.

She was seen on the *Vermont*, the *Swanee*, the *Decatur*,
the *Cape Romano*, the *Schuylkill*, the *Tulare*, and many
other ships. Some man on each one of them saw her. Not
everyone described her alike. To some she seemed tall, to
others short, to some pretty, to others plain. Most of them
noticed the glorious color of her hair. All of them remembered the deep throb of her voice. Few of them ever
called her beautiful but they remembered the light in her
eyes. Often the description was much like that of the
woman they knew best, missed most, and hungered after.

* * *

Sonnen was purser on the chartered transport *Curleigh.*
He had his room right behind his office. It held a six-foot
bunk, a little shelf with books, a small built-in wardrobe,

and a washstand. There was just floor space enough for
one man standing. For Sonnen, who liked to lie on his
bunk reading, it was a pleasant retreat.

There he could relax and know himself the luckiest
man on the ship, the only person below deck who had
solitude, the rarest and most prized possession on the
Curleigh.

Sonnen had been purser on her for three years before
the war, on northern runs in summer, on tropical cruises
in winter. Then his work had never let up. Today, the
passengers the *Curleigh* carried, as many soldiers as could
be packed on bunks five tiers high in three holds, were not
his concern.

Command lines were complicated on the *Curleigh.* An
Army colonel who couldn't stand the smell of human
vomit was in charge of the men. He stayed topside and
let his junior officers worry. They worried about the food,
the sick, the lack of air, the toilets which clogged every
hour and overflowed. These were maritime problems beyond any junior army officers. They attended to the various drills and inspections and ordered constant latrine
duty for men who could scarcely stand, but that was about
all they could do.

There was Navy aboard too—a gun crew under a lieutenant j.g., who, before the war, used to teach English
with emphasis on the Elizabethan poets. Some of the
junior army officers spoke to him, but he had his own
problems and jurisdiction only over his own crew.

In command of the ship was the Merchant Marine captain who ignored any problem except the one he felt
uniquely his, getting the ship to its secret destination.
His only concern was with the bridge and, except for
conferences with his engineer, with nothing animate or
inanimate below decks.

With each hour more of the cargo became inanimate.
The number of the troops that were staggered alphabeti-
cally for an hour topside in the morning and again in the
afternoon grew smaller each day.

It was a situation and no one could do much about it.

The men were needed at their destination, the *Curleigh* was the only transport available, and that was the way it was, as inevitable as the blackout battened-hatch order at night or the hot sun by day or the eternal motion of the ship which, on calmest days, resembled a corkscrew going through peanut brittle.

Sonnen, the purser, had learned one profound lesson from his years of experience, that there is little you can do about overcrowded ships at sea once the ship has sailed. He sat in his little office all day. In a sense, he was an anomaly on a ship in wartime but he neither knew the word nor would have cared if he had. This wartime cargo was human; its enumeration and listing was done by others. He had some paper work for the ship but no great amount. Although he always looked busy, much of his time was spent reading Westerns.

From the moment the ship cast off he had decided that what went on in the holds was none of his business. The stench annoyed him and the continuous coughing and retching at night, but most of the time he kept his door closed and heard it only as a distant and dim noise.

But the young lieutenants, whose O.C.S. had included no course on handling nine hundred seasick, green-faced, cursing, nauseated, bitching, homesick, stinking men, soon found his office. They began to hang around it and, shortly thereafter, to ask for advice.

"If you don't know what to do with your men," Sonnen said with great superiority, "get your goddam colonel down. Let him hand out perfume and bicarb and get everything sweet again."

Merkel, the youngest of the second lieutenants, took it hardest. He made valiant efforts to get better food served, to get the plumbing working. He had one of the few cabins topside and could breathe fresh air but he preferred to stay down with his men through all the day and much of the night. Because no one seemed to him to care, he cared all the more. He turned desperately to Sonnen.

"Do you know where we're going?" he asked.

"Sure," Sonnen said, "it's my business to know."

"How much farther have we to go?"

"Plenty," Sonnen said with no particular interest.

"Most of the men are sick."

Sonnen shrugged his shoulders. "That happens."

"But why in the name of the purple-striped Christ should we land with our men so sick they won't be worth a damn for three months?"

"Buddy, I don't run the Army. You do."

"Me?" Merkel ground a butt under his heel. "I wish I did. I wish to Christ I did for about five minutes."

"That's what all soldiers say sooner or later. Probably even your fat colonel up above wishes that now and then."

"Son of a bitch! He's only made one inspection."

"That's enough," Sonnen said casually. "He knows the men are on board."

Merkel shook his head. "Isn't there anything on God's earth that can be done for them?"

"Lieutenant," Sonnen said pompously, "we aren't running a twelve-day Caribbean cruise with all the comforts of home, including an eager schoolteacher, thrown in."

"Goddam!" Merkel shook his head and went away. Sonnen was very glad to see him go. Complaints annoyed him. Soldiers annoyed him. The war annoyed him. If there hadn't been a war, he would have been purser by now on one of the company's larger ships, with pleasant cruises in winter and his pick of the feminine passenger list. But the war brought cargoes of ammo and soldiers to be lugged all over the seven seas on trips as uncomfortable as this one.

Merkel returned every few hours. His anger at the colonel swelled over each mile of ocean.

"The fat can," he said this time. "It's funny how a man doesn't change. Back in the States he was always spit and polish—he heard somewhere that colonels get promoted on the basis of the amount of brass polish and shoe polish his men requisition. And that's all he cares about, being a general. Then, when the war's over, he goes back to his advertising agency and toothpaste accounts and 'generals' all his clients to death."

Sonnen had no special use for the colonel but found himself defending him. "What the hell—what can he do?"

"Can't you do something?"

"Me? I got nothing to do with colonels."

"But if you went to the captain of the ship?"

"He'd tell me to get the hell out, and damn right too."

"But if someone would show an interest, what could be done?" Merkel insisted.

"Food could probably be improved and the plumbing too."

"Well—"

"Well, Lieutenant, neither you nor I rank high enough. Get your goddamned colonel to take an interest."

Merkel looked helpless. "He's too busy with a gin rummy contest."

"Then for Christ's sake, don't bother me."

Merkel looked even more desperate. "Goddam it, there must be some way to stir you guys up."

Sonnen looked at him with real hostility. "We don't need any stirring up. Take it easy, like your other officers."

"One boy died this morning."

"He'd probably have died anyway. Where you guys are going, maybe he's lucky."

Merkel stared at him with all the anger he could mount and walked out. Sonnen smiled. Now maybe he could get some peace and go on with his reading.

He had peace, until that evening. Merkel returned to report another dozen men desperately ill, but Sonnen scarcely looked up from his book. A little later, Corcoran, the chief engineer, dropped in. Sonnen knew what he came for. From time to time he had a bottle hidden under his bunk. There was one there now, but he'd be damned if Corcoran would have any of it.

"Finished the last bottle last night," he told Corcoran innocently.

"Damned liar," Corcoran said. "Sometimes it's hard to know who I dislike more, the Army or the men out of it who ought to be in it." He left, growling in thirst and anger.

A few minutes later Sonnen heard a sound at his door but did not look up, sure it was the engineer back with his thirst and credulity still unsatisfied.

"Excuse me," Sonnen heard a woman's voice say, "but do you know a sailor aboard named Johnny Smith?"

Sonnen dropped his book and stared up at her. First he reacted automatically to the question. "No, never heard of him." Then he exploded, "What the hell? What'cha trying to do, get me in trouble?"

He jumped to his feet but at that moment she was gone. He blinked, looked around, then almost stumbled to his cabin and looked there. With the deepest bewilderment on his face he stepped toward the companionway. When he saw no trace of the girl his bewilderment changed to fear and concern. And, on the half trot down the companionway, came both the engineer and Merkel. Each looked angry.

"Who's the blonde that went into your office?" the engineer demanded, glad he had something on Sonnen.

"I saw her too," Merkel said.

"Don't ask me," Sonnen said. "She scared the hell out of me." He decided quickly it was best to join the side of the mystified rather than of the hurt and innocent.

"She went in your office."

"I heard a voice," Sonnen protested. "I looked up, saw a dame, and then she disappeared." He was trying desperately to be believed.

Both the engineer and Merkel showed him clearly they believed nothing.

They pushed him aside, strode into his little office and then into his cabin.

The engineer came out, his face black. "You've gotten away with plenty on this ship, Sonnen, and if you've got a woman on board—"

"My God!" Sonnen protested. "Where would I keep a woman?"

"I wouldn't put it past you if you could work it," the engineer snapped.

"She could be a stowaway of some sort," Merkel said.

"In any case, this is military security and I'm taking it to the colonel."

"Of course you should," Sonnen agreed uneasily.

"And I'm taking it to the captain," the engineer added.

"Sure," Sonnen said in the same uneasy tone, certain that he would catch hell from at least one direction and wanting to be on the right side at once. "Sure, we ought to take it to him right away."

The three started topside.

The next afternoon Sonnen sat slouched at his desk, still smarting from what the captain had said to him, and weary from a night spent helping to search the ship.

Merkel came in with the deepest, most satisfied smile on his face.

Sonnen looked up at him sourly. "Yeah, I know. Don't tell me."

"Boy, that captain of yours sure turned the ship upside down," Merkel said, satisfied.

"Your colonel was right behind him. I never saw such a worried man."

"Hell, one report of such a security breach and that guy'd be lucky to have even chickens on his shoulders, let alone stars."

Sonnen yawned. "Generals! Hell, we used to carry an old one regularly before the war every winter. Used to give his wife sleeping pills at night so he could get up on deck with the schoolteachers."

Merkel was still grinning. "It took the ghost of a dame to bring both of 'em down below and then when they saw what they saw!" His grin broadened. "The colonel had all he could do to keep from getting sick, just at the smells."

"Well, you got what you want," Sonnen said. "More air, and all that."

Merkel agreed. "Even the toilets are working now!" He thought about that for a moment. "But what gets me is, where did the dame come from?"

"Damn if I know. I heard of guys seeing all kinds of things when they're tired."

"I don't care either," Merkel said, "but I wish we could

count on her coming around every time the colonel needs
a kick in the pants."

*   *   *

The lights were out in Ward H on the hospital ship
Humanity. From a doorway at one end of the long narrow room came the weakest beam of light that barely
showed the two rows of beds.

It was dark in the room but the darkness was alive.
A fan whined just outside the door. Sometimes a bed
squeaked or the harness holding up a leg or arm rattled.
The beds in the ward were filled, and the men in them
lay asleep or at least motionless. Several men snored
gently. Under the sounds of the room was a deep formless voice, of ship and engines, the throbbing of a generator. And under that, felt rather than heard, was the
beat of the screws.

At the entrance was a little table with a green light
over it. Holton, a young nurse, sat there, tired at the
end of a long watch. Her paper work was done and put
aside. A novel at her elbow was too burdensome to open.
One hour more and she would be relieved, but the long-
est hour was the last one, and looking at her watch every
four minutes only chopped its length into small measured pieces.

At the far end of the ward, in the bed on the right,
nothing showed but a human shape under a sheet.
The man there had no idea of time. Time did not bother
him. He rested easily on it and cared nothing about its
passing, the speed of its passing, or its artificial division
into day and night. So long as it was there as a support
nothing else about it mattered.

Place did not trouble him. He was comfortable wher-
ever he was, and he thought no more about that.

What bothered him as restlessly as sand in a wound
was the unconnected continuity of events as they showed
in his mind. In a mind that felt no pain and a body that
lay in hungerless ease, he struggled, sometimes in half
sleep, sometimes in vague wakefulness, to connect the

pictures that passed in front of him. It was as if he had collected scraps of film from a hundred different movies and had pasted them together in an endless chain. Again and again this ran brightly through his mind.

It had already run a thousand times. Sometimes the scenes repeated themselves without change. Sometimes they were changed in details. Sometimes a new scene appeared, not to reappear again. He put all his strength to understanding their meaning, identifying them. He desperately needed to relate them to himself.

In one scene he saw a house with a sloping lawn. The house, with gables and porches, looked run-down and scaled with peeling paint. From time to time an unknown girl appeared on the porch. He was in this scene, cutting the grass from a lawn that never seemed to end. More irritating, so long was the swath he had to cut that by the time he came back to the beginning the grass had grown again on the places he had just cut. Worst of all, at times the lawn and the house with it tilted. Whenever he found himself at the end of the lawn, with the whole thing tilting precariously, he had to drive the mower deep into the grass to hold his balance and keep on his feet.

Or a man in Army uniform was dancing somewhere with a girl in a low-ceilinged room. The soldier was in the center of a cleared floor. Hundreds of eyes were watching from a blacked-out circle round about. The soldier did not know the girl and had nothing to say to her, but all those eyes were watching and the ears behind them were waiting for the soldier to say something and he could think of nothing to say, all the while he danced and whirled and whirled.

Or there was a cottage with a tall chimney. A girl stood at the cottage door watching the smoke rise upward, and he knew she was there because he could look down on her.

The smoke had carried him up and lifted him in great clockwise spirals skyward. Then the spiral reversed and lowered him almost to the chimney. Then reverse again, and he was borne upward while the girl, who seemed to

be the same girl in all the various pictures, watched him
without a smile.

Now and then there was something familiar in the
continuity. In one scene he was in his own home and
everything was familiar and in its place, from the blue
mat in the bathroom to the cigarette burns on the bridge
table that was stored in the front-hall closet. But the
house was crowded with people, all strange, with not one
familiar face among them. There were many people and
they had made themselves at home in his own living
room and dining room. When he walked through his own
home the strangers ignored him. They said nothing. They
answered no questions. In his own house, where everything was as he had always known it, there were only
strangers.

The same unknown girl was among them. As always,
she did not speak.

Other pictures and incidents followed, all disquieting,
inexplicable. Sometimes they repeated in the same order,
sometimes with no order. Viewing them continually, he
felt strained and fatigued as he struggled to use every last
erg of energy to understand them in terms of himself.

Now and then the pictures stopped. Formless mists
drifted through his mind and he could rest. The mists had
neither menace nor meaning and were without shape or
color. They had only motion and that was restful.

At the door to the ward Holton, the nurse, rubbed her
hands over her eyes. Hearing a man moan, she was on her
feet in an instant and moved quietly to a bed near by.
The man moaned again but he was asleep and she did
not disturb him. She returned to her chair.

The man at the far end of the ward, in the bed on the
right, could only reach one conclusion, that he was insane, that that was the only meaning to be gathered from
these unrelated and senseless views of a world in which
he had no place, no tie. Yet to deduce insanity in himself logically was in itself proof that he could not be
insane.

Then he heard a woman's voice, a voice familiar and

friendly, say, "Do you know a sailor named Johnny Smith on board this ship?"

"Yes, yes." He knew he was trying to sit up and that something held him down. He wanted to cry out happily. Here was the girl who had been in all those troubling scenes, here, beside him, alive and real and reassuring. His worries went and a whole real world came back. "Of course," he repeated. "Johnny Smith, that's me! Private Johnny Smith, Ninth Army Corps."

"Johnny Smith, a sailor, from South Dakota?" the same lovely voice asked.

"Johnny Smith, that's right, but I come from Bromide, Oklahoma, and I'm a soldier." He felt a hand touch him. "Sure. And who are you, miss?"

"Oh, Johnny!"

He knew she was gone without knowing how he knew. The room was too dark to see anything clearly and he felt too tired to be concerned. It did not matter now. She had been here and she would be back. To know that she was here and was real was enough.

Yet, near by, somewhere, someone was moving around. He spoke quietly, "Hello, hello!"

"Hello, soldier." It was Holton. Her voice was strong and cheering. "Feeling better?"

"Where did she go? Who are you?"

"I'm the nurse."

"Nurse? Where am I?"

"On shipboard, soldier, going stateside."

"Oh!" For a long while Smith was silent. "Oh, yes, I remember now. We were on a landing barge—I remember that. But that's all I remember." Then he asked very quietly, "Am I badly hurt?"

"Not so bad. You'll be all right."

"Yes," he said with sure conviction. "Of course I will."

"Good. Now get more rest. Is there anything I can bring you?"

"No. No thanks." Then, almost shyly, he asked, "Where's the other nurse, the one who was here?"

"Another nurse?" Holton did not hide her surprise.

"She came and called me by name. And she touched me."

Very gently Holton asked, "Are you sure?"

"Of course I'm sure. I couldn't see her very well because it's awfully dark here, but I really saw her."

"We have to keep it dark."

"I'd like to talk some more to that girl. I liked her voice. And she knew my name."

"Tomorrow, perhaps," Holton said. "Good night."

She returned to her desk with a puzzled look on her face. She was used to having patients report illusions and believe them. This was probably just another one but what troubled her even more was a half certainty that she too had heard a strange woman's voice. As for the boy—for a moment she rested her head on her arms, to tell herself for the thousandth time that in Army nursing, of all activities, feelings and emotions had always to be suppressed.

She was startled by footsteps. It was Corse, her relief, an older woman and an Army nurse long before the war.

Holton said, "Thank God you're here. Some of these night watches never seem to end."

"I know," Corse answered. "Anything new?"

"Nothing, except the Smith boy. I got him talking at last."

"Good. He's been in a coma ever since he was brought on board."

Then Holton said, after hesitating, "When he came to tonight he was sure some strange woman on board had been talking to him."

Corse nodded, as one who had heard stories like that before.

"The girl he wants to see most, no doubt. That's the commonest illusion these men have and, God knows, it's understandable."

Holton agreed but almost haltingly, "Yes. I suppose so. But I was sure I heard a woman's voice too."

Corse looked at her with hard professional skepticism.

"For just a moment I wondered if perhaps I'd fallen

asleep for a second," Holton confessed. "I was feeling very tired."

"Nonsense," Corse snapped.

As she gathered her things, ready to leave for the night, Holton said wearily, "The boy was awfully positive about it. Whatever it was, something brought him back to himself." She shook her head with the hourless fatigue that only nurses can know. "He even insisted that he'd seen her!"

That brought the faintest smile to Corse's face and erased all traces of doubt. "You'd better get to bed, Holton, and get a good night's sleep. Smith's the one who's totally blind, isn't he?"

*   *   *

Electrician's Mate Bowman, on the auxiliary vessel *Standholm,* was about as fine a workman as they come. On shipboard he was orderly, efficient, and more than reliable. On shore he had a hobby: women.

He always believed the old saying, "a sweetheart in every port," was the first commandment in the Sailor's Handbook. He added to that his own set of rules: "A guy's a sucker to have two dames in the same town at the same time." "The best thing to keep two different women apart is miles." "If you've had a dame once, well, you've had her." "The best cure for any mess is an outbound ship." These rules had worked so well that he went in and out of an affair like an amorous eel, with many dames, including Anna in New York, Helen in Boston, Marie in Baltimore, Louise in Seattle, Madeline in Los Angeles, Edna in Philadelphia. They had not yet been tried on the latest, Caroline in San Diego.

Bowman also had a wife and children in Norfolk, which had been home port for the *Standholm,* and he sent a large part of his money to them. He learned early that to get on with a dame a guy doesn't need money, only a bed, and more than half the time the dame will supply that. He was really generous with his family, and when the ship was in spent all his time with them.

Then the *Standholm* was transferred to the Pacific and based at San Diego. That was hard on his family but made things pleasanter for Bowman. That was where Caroline came in. In a way she reminded him of other women he had known. She was tall, like Margaret in Brooklyn, well built, like Jo in Camden, and as temperamental as Barbara in Savannah. She had her own unique qualities too, and looked Spanish. She was likewise as jealous as most of his dames had been. Bowman was something to be jealous of. At forty he was still attractive, slim and strong as turret steel. And he had the energy and endurance of a man of twenty-five, with the experience of a man of forty.

The *Standholm* was at sea one day when the mail came alongside. Bowman was used to a lot of letters. This time there were three. One was postmarked San Diego and had a return address in the 600 block on Arameda Street. It was from Caroline who said in eight pages that she couldn't wait until his ship got in again. The second was from Louise in Seattle to whom he had not written for some time. She said in one page that she knew damn well that his ship had been in Seattle and why hadn't he come around and if ever she met up with as much of a rat as he was she'd slit his throat. It made other threats and was not a very nice letter.

Bowman lingered over the letter from Caroline and reread it several times, smiling all the while. The letter from Louise he read once and tore into little pieces. He always did that with that sort of letter. He could never understand why dames should get so sore. After all, he never denied to any of them that he was married, and they ought to know better anyway than to mix up with a married man, and they deserved what they got, even if they got it from the married man himself. Thinking this way always made him feel righteous.

The third letter was from his wife. He opened it casually and began to read mechanically. It started:

Dear Phil: The children are well. I'm well, too. This letter will be a surprise to you. Look where we are—in San Diego. . . .

He stared at that line, then looked at the return address. It was "625 Arameda Street, San Diego." With the feeling of eyes popping, he raced through the rest of the letter. It continued:

> The Harrisons, remember our neighbors in Norfolk, had a brother in San Diego who was transferred to Norfolk. When I heard about that I agreed to swap houses because I knew you'd be happier with us in San Diego, now that your ship is based there.

There was more detail, about the trip across the country and how it had been financed, about the children's colds, and details about the new house. Bowman ignored all of them. All he knew was that his wife had acted most selfishly, to do this without telling him, and that she lived at 625 Arameda Street while Caroline lived across the street at 626. Right away that broke up the most promising friendship before it was ready to be broken up. And, more important, if his wife happened to meet Caroline, if one neighbor happened to mention his name— He felt cold just considering the various possibilities.

Helplessness at sea is real helplessness. There was the situation and there was nothing he could do to stop it developing, to guide or direct it. At this moment his wife might be meeting Caroline—if not this moment, then tomorrow, a week from now. For a little while he let himself think about his wife and what she would do. She would raise hell. She would probably not divorce him but she would keep the children from him and that would hurt more than anything. And worse of all, she could wreck his ego—he who was always so careful to arrange everything just right by a time-tested series of rules.

That letter spoiled his day. He had a dirty job to do on a generator and fussed and fumed over it. He dropped a wrench on his foot, which did not help. And his two assistants caught a lot of unusual abuse for their stupidity and clumsiness.

One of them asked, "What in hell's wrong with Bowman?"

"God knows," the other said. "Probably a couple of

his dames wrote him that unless he marries them they'll
write the Secretary of the Navy."

Bowman ate supper in silence, his feeling of helplessness increasing by the minute. He continued to think of
his wife and what she might do and was surprised to find
himself really concerned. Maybe he felt more deeply
about her than he realized. Of Caroline he scarcely
thought. He was prepared to sacrifice her at once on the
altar of compulsory faithfulness, and while that was re-
grettable, there were probably still dames around Long
Beach or Honolulu.

At evening he felt he had to do something. He could
do little against the grinding mills of coincidence, but
to do anything would relieve in small part the sense of
helplessness that was so crippling. He got a pad of writing paper and sat down to do some letters. They needed
careful thinking and his quarters were too noisy. He went
off to the galley, found an empty corner and a table, and
began a first letter. With that he had little trouble. It
was to Caroline and he had written many like it before.
With great regret and many reminders of how happy
they had been, he hated to have to announce that he had
been transferred to another ship that would be based
somewhere else, far off. He couldn't even write any more
until he knew his new address. Many a long day would
pass before he'd be back in San Diego, and so on.

It was a complete and moving letter of regretful re-
nunciation. As he finished it he decided that she probably
wouldn't feel so bad.

After all, if she'd mixed up with him, she'd mix up with
others like him and shouldn't have it too tough finding
his successor.

Then he wrote his wife, but only after thinking carefully. He decided there was nothing he could really say—
just a pleasant friendly letter. He wrote that he was really
glad she was on the West Coast and particularly on Arameda Street in San Diego, a part of the city he happened
to know well. He smiled as he wrote that. When he'd be

ashore next he didn't know, but maybe soon, and he was glad the kids were well and he'd see them soon.

Now he could relax a little. That was all he could do and maybe, with the luck that had never deserted him yet, he would have to do nothing else, except to do some skillful dodging around Caroline's house when he was ashore.

He decided to mail the letters at once and started back to his quarters to get envelopes.

He went along a dark companionway, deeply immersed in his own worries and somewhat sorry that land worries should follow so far out to sea. Suddenly he heard a woman's voice say something about knowing a certain sailor.

He was much too astonished to hear correctly, let alone answer. He wavered and stepped back because there, five feet off, was a woman with blond hair. The woman and the voice were not imagined. He stepped forward, arms out ready to ward off anything, but there was nothing there.

He continued slowly down the corridor, unable to control the shaking of his hands. When he came to his quarters he sat down hard on his bunk and for some minutes found it impossible to move.

Men around him were asleep, but several pals noticed him.

One of them said, "What's the matter, Phil? You look as if you'd seen a ghost."

"Just a headache," he mumbled.

Obviously, what he had seen, he told himself, was an illusion of some sort, to be seen by any overtired and overworried man. No one else had seen it, and any tired man could be forgiven for seeing things at night. Yet he made himself question that: he had been tired many times before, and worried, but never had he had such an experience.

The girl, if it was a girl, was a blonde, and resembled in a way many he had known, particularly Barbara in Savannah, and Louise in Seattle. They had both written to him their sharp opinion of him and had added miscellaneous threats. Barbara had even written, "If ever you do me dirt, I'll haunt you."

He sat up and managed to make his hands cease trembling. He told himself that what he was thinking was all nonsense, dreadful, empty, meaningless nonsense, but that did not stop the fast current of uncontrolled thought now rushing through his mind. Then common sense told him that these women were far, far away and that nothing but the unexpected news of the day was responsible for the whole bewildering experience. Everything would pass with a good night's sleep. For a moment he felt better, then knew he was kidding himself. No troubles would pass until the situation in San Diego was settled or, at least, its development known. At this minute some neighbor might be saying, "Caroline, I do want you to meet a newcomer from the East, Mrs. Bowman. Her husband is an electrician's mate in the Navy."

And his wife would see the look that would break out on Caroline's face.

He reached into his locker and got the envelopes. Still concerned and realizing he was more worried than he even knew, he absent-mindedly addressed the envelope to his wife and the envelope to Caroline.

Or at this moment a neighbor might be saying, "Funny, Mrs. Bowman, but that girl across the street used to have a caller named Bowman, an electrician's mate, quite a good-looking man of forty."

Concentrating on all the things that might be happening, that could happen, Bowman carefully put his wife's letter in Caroline's envelope and vice versa and sealed them most carefully.

Still wondering, however, why one man's peaceful life should become so infernally complicated through no fault of his own, he went off to the mailbox and posted the letters.

They would help, he told himself as he turned back to his quarters. No matter how tight the situation, all a man had to do was to keep his nerves steady. He even laughed now at his own nervousness in thinking he had seen a ghost.

*   *   *

Most of Chief Petty Officer Joe Jones's friends who were with him on the *Farragut* wouldn't know him now. When he was transferred to the *Louisiana* they gave him quite a send-off. They said enviously, "Lucky guy, Joe, landing on the newest battlewagon in the Navy. But that won't make any difference to Joe. Nothing changes him."

The *Louisiana* is the biggest thing afloat. According to Joe, after he returned from the shakedown cruise, she uses ordinary destroyer escorts swung from davits for lifeboats and tows a small carrier to serve as captain's tender. Without revealing any military secrets, Joe went into some detail about her speed. She moves so fast that they put the plane catapults at the stern because when she's moving at full speed the planes flip off backward even with their motors at full gun.

Her captain runs a tight ship, Joe said, just the way he himself likes a ship run, and nothing escapes him. At inspection one morning the Old Man stared at a couple of seamen's feet and told them to take off their shoes. Sure enough, their socks had holes in them.

That's Joe! Of his pride in his new ship he said nothing except that it was the best goddam far-flung, french-fried, fine-feathered, fast-flitting, fresh-frizzled, fancy-fandango of a ship in the whole fouled-up, fouled-out, fouled-to-a-full-fare-thee-well Navy.

When they commission a new ship like the *Louisiana*, they put a lot of new men on her, fresh from boot camp. Then they salt them heavily with men like Joe Jones, twenty-five years in the Navy, with so many hash marks on their sleeve they list to starboard. Men like Joe have forgotten more about the sea and ships than a lot of admirals know. The one-stripers can strut around as if they run the ship, and the gold braid may think they run her, but the chief petty officers know damn well who really makes her go.

The best of them remember when they were just apprentice seamen and couldn't tell a porthole from a coffee pot. And the very best of them, like Joe, keep as close a personal contact with the men under them as any clucking hen. One way Joe did it was to join any group of seamen he saw sitting off duty. At first they would feel awkward and stop talking out of shyness or something like that. Later, they likewise stopped talking but because Joe never gave them a chance. He talked only about one thing, the Navy. And much of what he said was critical. The Navy was not perfect and never would be. But a man needn't be blamed for wanting it that way.

"When I joined up in 1917," he told a gang one night, "there was none of the careful training you boots get today. My God, I even hear they give you swimming lessons. In my time you were dumped off the stern of whatever ship you happened to be on and you damn well swam."

"What if the ship was moving?"

"Half the time it was. I remember one fellow who was pushed off the old *Pennsylvania* when she was moving full speed ahead. Guy couldn't swim a stroke."

"What happened to him?"

"We were sure he was drowned."

"Was he?"

Joe was waiting for that question. "No, sir." He lit a cigarette, "that's where we were wrong. Seems that he landed in the wake close to the screws. Instead of pulling him under they set him spinning like a torpedo. He shot backwards, right through the water, spinning round and round and doing about three knots an hour. He had enough sense to grab for air every time his mouth came up. He was still turning but at a reduced speed when a following destroyer sighted him and picked him up, but not before the lookout sang out, 'Torpedo off starboard bow!' And a funny thing, and you don't have to believe it—"

"What?"

"His hair turned curly as a result of all that twisting

around. In fact, still is." Joe looked over his audience
for any show of disbelief and saw none. "If any of you
men ever run into anyone from the *Kansas City* ask about
Chief Petty Officer Curly McKibben. They'll tell you.
And don't take my word for it either."

He pulled on his cigarette for a moment.

"What do we get today?" he said, scoffing. "A nice
swimming pool with water six feet deep. They even warm
it, I hear."

Joe waited but no one cared to dispute it.

"In fact," he continued, "we don't even get the same
kind of men. Today what do they send us from boot
camp? Children, and gummers' mates."

"What the hell is a gummer's mate?"

Joe asked disgustedly, "Don't you guys know nothing?
I'll tell you what a gummer's mate is. He's one of those
guys who come in the Navy with bad teeth so they give
him new plates, topside and below. He goes to sea and
doesn't like it. When the ship's heading in, what does he
do? Tosses his plates overboard. Then when he gets
ashore he says the plates slipped over by accident and he
has to have a new set and that's the way he gets four weeks
on shore while he's being fitted. But don't none of you
guys try it unless you want to cruise around for a while
eating nothing but oatmeal."

He let that sink in before going on. "Gummers' mates
and children! Children! Let 'em have a couple hours
liberty and where do you find 'em. At bars? No, sailor, at
hamburger stands, drinking pop and milkshakes and eating hot dogs. Don't any of you ever stop to think what
a mixture like that'll do to your stomachs? Any day now
the sick bay'll need a sailor for a transfusion and when
they tap him they'll find his veins run chocolate milkshakes."

Joe showed his disgust on his face. "Not like the old
days. Today sailors go ashore and stay sober and then God
knows what trouble they get into. In the old days when a
sailor went ashore he headed for a bar, stayed till he got
dead drunk and dropped. Then you always knew where

to find him and you'd find he hadn't gotten into any un-
foreseen trouble at all.

"If ever you get aboard the *Squantum,* you ask about
Hokie Cassell. I guess he's still aboard. There's the last
of the old-fashioned sailors left in the Navy. He says he
helped swab down the guns at Manila in '98, but he
always was pretty much of a liar except where drinking
was concerned, and you can't believe all he tells you. But
what a man! Steadiest hand at a wheel you ever saw. A
skipper once found him sailing two degrees off course,
and after they dragged him up before the mast they
found, so help me, and you don't have to believe it, they
found the compass was wrong."

Joe lit a cigarette before he went on. "But the best
story about Hokie is the time we were in Boston, laid up
for a couple of weeks. He decided that was enough time
for a really good drunk so he went out to get it. For four
days he just drank and drank and what do you expect of
a man—on the fifth day he just dropped, right where he
was, in Coogan's bar, just back of the Navy Yard. Well,
Coogan didn't know what to do with him so he turned
him over to the police, just friendly like, not as an arrest,
but just for thoughtful loving care. The police knew
Hokie so they put him down in the basement of a station
house so he could sleep it off. I heard he slept forty-one
hours without moving but that seems like a hell of a long
time.

"Anyway, he woke up some time and when he did it
was black dark. He put one hand overhead and felt the
bunk above. Then he felt to one side and there was
boards. Then he felt underneath and there he felt boards
too."

Joe stopped to let that sink in.

"Well, he came to a simple conclusion and you couldn't
blame him. At the top of his voice he yelled, 'Dead, goddam it, dead and buried!' He just couldn't believe it, so
he reached down again and touched the boards and he
grunted, 'And what a hell of a note—buried on land.'
Then he reached down once more and got a long splinter

in his finger. That's when he really roared, and they heard him through the whole police station, 'Buried, and buried goddam cheap!'

"Yes, sir, there was a sailor. You get on the *Squantum* some time, you ask about Hokie. But don't offer him nothing to drink." With that, Joe got up and walked away.

That was the way Joe used to be, but he changed on board the *Louisiana*. Not even his old friends would know him now.

One night a gang was hanging around and the conversation came to Waves and women in the Navy. Joe told what he thought of them. "The last time I was ashore," he said, "I went to the Paymaster's Office to straighten up some mixup with my pay. The paymaster was an old pal of mine and yet he said he couldn't help—something about having to send more papers to Washington. Right then, along came a Wave who worked in the office and damn if she didn't know the answer and how to fix things right off. The Navy'll go to hell if women have the right to put a guy on a spot like that and that paymaster's been in the Navy a long time. He took it hard."

Joe shook his head. It was a serious matter.

Some ordinary and simple seaman said, "I don't think Waves are so bad. I even met one once I could marry."

"Not bad?" Joe exploded, not used to contradictions. "Then let me tell you—women around ships are just a menace." He lowered his voice. "They even have trouble with them working in the shipyards, I hear. When they were building the ship we're on, I heard one story about a woman welder who was working inside a fuel tank. Well, not until this scow was launched did they bother to check up and find she'd disappeared. They never saw her in the yard again."

"What happened to her?"

"Now, there's a stupid question for you," Joe said with disgust. "Any fool would know what happened. She welded herself inside the tank, that's what happened."

"Why didn't they open up the tank?"

"Which do you think ought to come first, sailor? Getting a battleship out on time or tearing down half of it to find a woman who was probably dead by that time?"

When there was no answer Joe said, "You don't have to believe that story at all, but some of the guys who were on the first trial runs heard some awful funny sounds. Pounding and scratching and a funny sort of voice. This wouldn't be the first ship in the Navy to be haunted."

With that he finished and walked away, congratulating himself on having made up a new story on the spur of the moment.

Late that night Joe wanted some coffee, of which he drinks about a gallon a day and always has. He was heading down the companionway to the galley, satisfied and content with himself, the ship, the world, and, even for the moment, with the Navy. He turned down a cross companionway, a sort of blind alley lined with locked closets. The blue lights made it very shadowy.

In the half darkness Joe heard something rustle. Then a voice said, "Excuse me, but do you know a sailor named Johnny Smith on board?"

That took Joe by surprise. He caught a glimpse of blond hair and a dress somewhere in front of him. He said, "What?" Then he said much louder, "What the hell!" Then he made a dive for the shadowed figure and grabbed exactly nothing.

"Listen, you smart sailor," he said, reaching out again and again into air.

Between Joe and the end of the companionway was about twenty feet of space, ending in a blind alley. There was no one there and no one, he was sure, could have slipped by him.

His first reaction was to sound an alarm, but years of experience made him cautious. This was something personal, between himself and the voice and he needed no help—and no ribbing from everyone aboard for having fallen for the best gag of the year.

When he could find no one he came back to the petty

officers' quarters but stayed only a moment. Then he headed topside to find a seaman, Simmons, who had been one of the group around when he told the story of the welder.

Joe found him and said, "I want you to think of all the guys who were with you this evening. Remember? Then chase around and see that they're in their bunks or accounted for. Hurry up!"

"Yes, sir," Simmons said obediently. He returned to report that four were on watch and six were in their bunks sound asleep.

"That's all of 'em?"

"That's all, sir."

"Do you know anyone—?" Then Joe realized he could not finish the question which had to do with knowing anyone who might have a woman's dress in his locker. It sounded far too silly to ask and was sure to lead to gossip around the ship and to eventual questions.

"You were asking?" Simmons said politely.

"Nothing, goddam it," Joe said, storming off.

And that was the end of Joe's yarn spinning and he hasn't come back to himself yet. For weeks he went around trying to match a voice he remembered with voices he heard. For weeks he went around trying to notice any trace of a hidden smile.

Joe hasn't mentioned the incident to anyone on the *Louisiana* but he did meet up with Petty Officer Norton from the *Forsythe* in a New York bar. They were old friends, had been apprentices together. After a couple of drinks Joe told him the story. "Sure, they were smart kids to think up that gag the very night I was kidding them about the ship being haunted. But what gets me is where in hell did they get that blond wig?"

*   *   *

To Lieutenant Stowell, standing watch on the bridge of the light cruiser *Koowell*, the path of the stars was always a thing of wonder. He knew them all and they

were his friends and, beyond that, they had been a tie
with Ellen, his wife.

On this night as on all other clear nights for the past
months Stowell did not go below when relieved, but
stood at the rail looking up at the sky, looking up steadily and contentedly. As long as he could remember, the
stars had been a part of his life as a favored hobby. In
boyhood he had lain on a grassy hilltop, naming them
and watching them swing their familiar way. He could
stand now and see Pegasus and remember how he saw
it for the first time in his life, coming brightly from the
northeast on a spring evening. When he looked up at the
star now, he thought, as always, of Ellen.

He heard a step on deck and frowned. He needed no
company at a time like this. His cabin-mate, Lieutenant
Porter, was coming up to him casually and nonchalantly.
He had roomed with Porter for a year, but had taken
few steps into the common ground of friendship. He
preferred to be reserved. Porter, on the other hand, a
hearty extrovert who lived from day to day, had at first
seemed to resent the reserve; now he accepted it and
rarely asked questions.

Yet he came up with a question. He asked, "Star gaz-
ing as usual, Hal?"

"Hello," Stowell said colorlessly.

Porter stood beside him. "They fascinate you, don't
they?"

Stowell nodded.

For a long time Porter waited without a word. From
below came the soft liquid noise of the ship in the waters.
Finally, in almost petulant impatience, he said, "Hal, it's
none of my business but we do bunk together and I like
you. Is anything wrong?"

In a quiet and thoroughly controlled voice Stowell
asked, "Why should anything be wrong?"

Porter went ahead like a man who had taken up an
unpleasant job but was determined to go through with
it. "You've changed so much in the last four months, ever
since your wife's death."

"It was a shock."

"Of course it was," Porter agreed heartily, finding sympathy easier than interrogation.

Stowell turned from the sky for the first time. "I know what you want to say. 'See here, Hal old man, you just can't spend your life in mourning.' Isn't that it?" But before Porter could answer he asked coldly, "Have you heard any criticism of my work on this ship?"

"On the contrary," Porter answered hastily, "just the other day I heard the Old Man say you were one of the most valuable men he'd ever had."

The small spark of Stowell's anger had not lasted long. "I don't think I could explain to anyone what Ellen meant to me. I never knew any other woman, never wanted any other woman. Maybe we lived too close and that makes it tougher, but I wouldn't have had it any other way."

The sudden flow of confidence made Porter feel slightly uneasy. He said, "It must be difficult to think of going back home some day."

"It's not that," Stowell said. "I'm quite at peace with myself about that. I'm Naval Reserve but if they'll let me stay on after the war I'm in the Navy for life."

"Not to go back to teaching, ever? Boy, I can't wait to get out."

Stowell shook his head. "I've decided I'll be happier at sea." He continued firmly, "I just can't face picking up life ashore without Ellen. At least I don't suffer from uncertainty about the future. I'm quite at peace about that. I like the Navy and I'll stay on if they'll have me."

That more than satisfied Porter. He felt relieved and said so. "I'm glad to know what's been on your mind, Hal. Personally, I saw you so much by yourself that I began to worry and you know me, I never worry. You'll excuse me for intruding—"

"I'm grateful to you for your concern," Stowell said sincerely. He turned again to the stars, and Porter, standing by, felt as if he had gone off somewhere. He decided to go below and was about to leave when Stowell said,

"I don't suppose there are many marriages like Ellen's and mine."

"I don't suppose there are many happy marriages," Porter said.

"You hear a lot about sailors and girls in every port," Stowell said slowly. "But I never could see it. I think it's unfair to a lot of good Navy men too."

"Probably," Porter agreed.

"Now and then you hear a story about men," Stowell said earnestly, "that just baffles me. Maybe 'baffle' is too weak a word. Were you in the wardroom the other night when Ensign Brown was telling about his last leave?"

"I missed it," Porter said, "but I can imagine. Some of his stories are pretty juicy."

"He told about going to a reception after a wedding. It must have been quite a party. The bridegroom got drunk and passed out somewhere so the bride insisted that Brown come to bed with her because she didn't want to sleep alone on her bridal night. And he did."

"I heard something about that one," Porter admitted. "But that concerns a woman as much as a man."

"I don't want to pass judgment," Stowell continued. "I just want to say that I can't understand a thing like that. Look," he said, his voice deepening in concern, "I never seemed to fit in the world until I met Ellen. I was always solitary and didn't like people. She had so much grace and charm she just made me fit, or maybe she provided me with a world into which I could fit." He stopped for a moment. "Funny, I haven't been able to speak about her until tonight."

Porter felt that he was now eager to talk about her.

"We met in college," Stowell went on. "Even in our sophomore year we had our marriage planned and I planned how I would get a job as instructor and how she would open a nursery school. And we planned our house —that took junior and senior year—Ellen had a little money so we knew what we could do. We even planned a place for a little telescope because Ellen knew how crazy I was about stars and she was interested in them too."

Again his voice took on a deep emotional tone. "Then we graduated and we built the house and I got the job as instructor and she opened a nursery school, all as we planned, and I never thought of another woman through all those years."

He stopped for a moment and looked far out to the horizon. "Then the war came and I felt I had to join the Navy. I didn't have to go—I could have stayed and done research in physics and have been deferred. I felt I had to go. There was never any question in my mind or hers about the rightness of that. She just said, 'No wife has any right to ask her husband to live for her alone. If he has talent it belongs as much in the world as it does in a close-bound family and it must be used there.'" Stowell coughed for a moment. "That was what she said."

Porter listened closely, feeling that this had been long dammed up in Stowell and had to come out. He marveled at the man's quietness.

"Then, four months ago, she was killed in an auto accident," Stowell was saying.

Porter wished he could reach out with some open, wide gesture of sympathy, but he could say nothing.

Stowell was asking a question and Porter missed it. He said, "I beg your pardon?"

"Do you think there's anything after death?" Stowell repeated.

"I haven't thought much about it," Porter said clumsily. "If you pin me down, I suppose I don't believe in much of anything."

"Do you really think death can end the sort of relationship Ellen and I had?" Stowell asked even that question unemotionally.

His tone of voice made Porter uncomfortable. He usually did little thinking beyond plans for tomorrow or for the next leave. He answered, "I suppose most people would say so."

"And most people would be wrong," Stowell said, a deep note of triumph in his voice. "For one thing, as long as I am alive it can't die. That's a comfortable thought sometimes—we can give the person we loved an immortality of a sort in our own minds. And with me and Ellen it goes beyond that." He took Porter firmly by the arm and swung him around. "Look up there, at that bright star. Know its name? It's Pegasus. It's always been a favorite of mine. When I was ready to leave home Ellen said—it was like her to think of it—'Look up at Pegasus every night and I'll do the same. Then perhaps by going millions of miles away we can be close for a moment.'"

Porter began to feel slightly troubled. There was a new firm tone to Stowell's words.

Then Stowell lowered his voice. "Since I've known of her death I haven't missed a night here and I get the strongest sense of her still being here, near by, strong, real, and unchanged, a solid presence."

Porter felt a strange feeling in his arms and throat.

"I probably couldn't make you believe that," Stowell added, "but I do know that I still have what was most precious of all, Ellen."

As he said those last words Porter was sure that he had forgotten that anyone was near by. He was talking to the deep blue sky, not to a man. And Porter felt thoroughly uneasy, knowing nothing he could say nor anything he wanted to say. As quickly as he thought polite he said, "Well, I'll be going below. Good night." He went on his way, deeply troubled.

His first reaction was to blame himself for poking into another man's private affairs. After regretting that, he tried to decide what should be done. His first impulse was to go to the ship's doctor for advice; but that would just be poking further into the same private affairs. Then he told himself that all men need some illusion if they are to go on living. Why do anything about Stowell? No one had complained about him and he was still a most satisfactory officer. Porter left the deck shaking his head wearily; he was no hand at complicated personal problems or psychopathic states. He was just grateful that he had none of his own.

He turned into the companionway to the officers' quarters.

He heard someone move and in the blue light he heard a woman's voice ask something about some sailor. He caught a glimpse of blond hair, a tall woman.

He put his hands to his eyes and wavered, sure for the moment that he was out of his mind. When he looked again the companionway was empty. He came to his cabin feeling dizzy and sat down on his bunk. A moment before he had been willing to think of Stowell as a harmless fool living on illusions. Now, with a sudden throat-jolting shock, he had seen an illusion and he was not so sure who was a fool. Stowell had been so quietly firm in his certainty that his wife was never far away, and all Porter could do was to shake his head wearily. Then he told himself that he was a fool to think that he had been the victim of anything more than an optical trick induced, perhaps, from looking up at the sky too long. In fact, that probably explained Stowell and his illusions.

Porter turned in. As he lay restlessly on his pillow he would not let himself admit that Stowell could be right, no matter if there had been the live shadow and the warm voice of a woman in the companionway. To admit that she had any more reality than a brain trick would be to widen the real and comfortable limits of Porter's world to something infinite, unknown, and shadowed. But in spite of himself, there was doubt in his mind, and he wanted desperately to know. Then he thought of a question he could ask Stowell, a question which would conclusively mark as a trick of the imagination whatever Porter thought he had seen. He lay awake until Stowell finally came to the cabin.

"Say, Hal!"

"Good Lord, you still awake?"

"I've been thinking about what you said on deck," Porter continued, trying to be casual. "You made your wife very real to me by what you said. I wish I'd known her." Then he asked, "What did she look like?" He knew the answer he hoped to hear.

He did not hear it. Stowell said, "She was tall and very blond."

"I thought she might be short and dark."

"No, tall and blond. G'night."

Thoroughly unsatisfied, Porter squirmed deeper under his blanket, wishing he had never opened any conversation with Stowell, wishing he were back in a tight and bright little world well within the margins of darkness.

*   *   *

Remember Tarawa and Okinawa? Sure, never to be forgotten. And the men who died there rest in the certain satisfaction that what they did will be remembered.

Remember Ulithi, Majuro, Abemama, Emirau? We invaded those too, spits of sand we had to have, and the men who died on their beaches are just as dead as the men who died at Iwo. On these forgotten islands they rest, and the sand packs tight around them while their friends have gone on to other islands, to die on other beaches. The little invasions, the crumbs of global warfare, eventually to be remembered only by mapmakers and mothers.

The Navy transport *Morton* was headed to one such little island, loaded to the gunwales with marines. They filled all the decks, packed like pickles in a bottle, bunked five high in the holds. The *Morton* was one of a convoy headed for Katana, too small to show on most maps except those of high strategy. Because the island had an airstrip on it, it had to be plucked off.

In the whitewashed hold on the second deck a young marine, Bill Gorman, was lying on his canvas bunk, second up from the floor. On the bunk below four of his friends sat talking. Their names are unimportant. You can find all of them in the sandy white cemetery on Katana.

"I heard one flier who'd done reconnaissance over Katana say he never saw so many gun emplacements put so close."

"Nuts. Probably coconut logs."

Gorman was nineteen and so proud of being a marine it stuck out like a permanently inflated chest. During his four years in high school he had given his family no peace. He wanted to be a marine. Now he was a marine and by dawn on the morrow he would know how good a marine he was.

Round about in the darkness were four hundred others. Now and then canvas bunks squeaked. The blower pipes never stopped humming but the hum of conversation was louder.

Gorman could not help hearing the group below him, but his own thoughts were far more vivid.

"What I say is that it's funny they haven't told us anything about how tough they expect this landing will be."

"That could mean it'll be a cinch. If they thought it would be tough, they'd tell us."

"What for? Better let us take it in our stride."

"Oh, sure."

Gorman turned on his canvas bunk, trying to find a more comfortable place for a tired back on the taut mattressless canvas. Here he was, in the hold of a transport, by way of Parris Island and Hawaiian jungle training. That was the path he had come, and every step thus far was sure and happy. To the slow roll of a transport, from the steadiness of an Iowa farm.

"Another guy was telling me that any day now they expect the Nips to use gas."

"Aw, nuts."

"What have they got to lose? If they got gas, and you can bet they have, why not use it? What have they got to lose? And they got the know-how."

"Sure, the don't-know-nothing-no-how."

Someone laughed. "If they use gas we'll put a guy with a mouth as big as yours on the beach and let his jaw flap the breeze and blow the gas right back at them."

"Aw, nuts."

Gorman stopped moving about and settled back. He took a stick of gum from his pocket and began to chew it. He listened, through the conversation below, to the

sounds of the ship. He had not yet learned to feel wholly
at ease on shipboard. But he knew all the earth sounds
and the feel of earth, whether mud, sand, or crusty road,
or the softness of new furrows.

"The way I figure it, if you got your name on a bullet,
you get it."

"Think that one up just now, all by yourself?"

"Maybe the Japs got all anonymous bullets."

"Aw, nuts."

At his small well-tramped crossroads of thought Gorman considered one thing again and again. Being on this
transport, its bow headed west and not far off Katana,
was like being at the end of something. Nothing more to
be learned, nothing more to be taught. Anything he
didn't know now might remain forever unknown. This
was it.

"Anyway, we got no weather worries."

"The Marines see to everything, bud."

"After what they put us through on Parris Island who
cares about the weather?"

"I'll say!"

Deep among the things in his mind was something that
puzzled Gorman. A dozen times during this dark evening
he had felt that he had been through all this earlier—
certainly not the same physical experience of lying here
five deep, while on deck above were landing nets piled
high and gear stacked on all sides. But in some way,
somehow, all this was a repetition of something known
and endured before.

"One thing about these invasions. They certainly send
along stuff."

"I'll say."

"The number of ships'll make the Japs think we really
mean to shovel the island aboard and cart it off."

"And a hell of a good idea that would be."

Through most of the evening Gorman had tried to
locate that feeling of repetition and to find why it all
seemed so very real. It was not because of repetition in
maneuvers. Whenever he had practiced the movements

of the hours ahead, the scampering down the landing nets, the lurch into the landing boats, the silent and surging ride to the shore, it had been like a game, rousing no particular deep feeling, and certainly nothing of the unidentified shadow he knew now.

"How many of these goddam little islands are there?"

"Plenty."

"Are the Marines gonna have to take 'em all? Why the hell don't they put all the energy into one big push and take Tokyo?"

"Listen to him—strategy from a guy who couldn't even call a hit-and-run play right in last Saturday's ball game."

The words "ball game" brought back a clear picture of high school to Gorman, and at once he remembered clearly where he had been through something like this before, this period of waiting, of forced freedom from the nervousness he knew was in him and in the voices of all the men below him and around him. At home, at high school, on Commencement morning! That was a silly comparison, he told himself, but for him it was real and precise. So much of it was alike, even to that funny feeling in the hands that seemed to perspire between the fingers as well as on the palms.

"I knew a guy who went in at Tarawa. He said his landing craft got stuck on a reef and he had to swim a couple hundred yards."

"Geez, I'd hate that. I hate walking around in wet clothes."

"If you get stuck on a reef you're lucky if you get a chance to walk."

For one thing, Commencement had that same sense of an end, of marking a moment when all there was to be learned had been learned. No more classes or study hours. And the same feeling, too, of being led to cliffside, to look down on a fog-wrapped unmarked world below. The same feeling of being close to a group of friends, bound with the tightest ties, and the same feeling that at a given moment these would be broken and never again would their world be as it was and as it had been.

"The guys that went in at Tarawa—"

"Hell, this thing tomorrow isn't going to be any Tarawa."

"It was the kind of soil they hit. They couldn't get started."

"Don't you think maybe the Nips had something to do with it?"

The Commencement exercises were at ten in the morning in the Grace Church auditorium because the high-school assembly room would not hold enough people. Gorman could remember all the preparations as if it were yesterday rather than a year ago: the vote for class flower, the discussions over what the boys should wear. They decided on blue serge coats and white flannel pants. He remembered how long he had stood at the mirror, debating over two neckties, and how pleased he was at what he saw in the mirror and how carefully he kept that pleasure submerged. He remembered his concern when he found that the crease on the left leg of the new white flannels threw the cuff a little to the side, and he recalled the hope that no one would notice it.

"By the time the fleet gets finished tomorrow morning we'll be lucky if there's enough of the island left to land on."

"Yeah? They blasted Tarawa for God knows how many days."

"They've been pounding Katana for two weeks with more ships and more shells."

"Besides, the Navy's got a shell now that's allergic to Nips and chases them until it hits them."

The whole senior class assembled in the Sunday School room. Gorman remembered wondering if he looked as uncomfortable and store-windowy in his serge and flannels as the other boys did. Everybody was kidding everybody else and he got more than his share. He was valedictorian, and a dozen times the boys said, "Boy, you'll feel rotten if you muff it." Or, "You can't imagine how you'll feel, talking up there. Don't try."

"I heard the Germans sent out all the plans for all un-

finished secret weapons and that the Nips have been working on them."

"Sure, that's right. Including the Y-for-goodness-sake."

"What's that one?"

"What the Nip yells when one of our flame throwers
hits him."

A dozen times that morning Gorman had reviewed the
opening of his speech. The introduction was complicated.
It went: "Mr. Coolson"—he was the principal—"Mr.
Congressman"—he was the Commencement speaker—
"faculty members, members of our families, fellow class-
mates." He almost always dropped one group out and
sweated when he thought of muffing that opening. After
that it went: "Today we stand at a threshold, the threshold that leads to the road of life." Even now, on this
slow swinging transport, he could remember most of that
speech. It ended: "So we are to say a valedictory, a fare-
well. But better, far better, I believe it if we say, instead,
'Greetings, we are here and we are ready.' "

"I wonder what the timetable for the whole thing is."

"Shouldn't be more than a week."

"A week, to take that piece of bird dropping?"

"You never can tell how tough—"

Someone called down from an upper bunk, "Why
don't you guys shut up and stop worrying?"

Four voices called back, "Who the hell's worrying?"

The class, Gorman remembered, filed onto the platform and sat down, each one watching the other to see
what he was doing with his hands. The Glee Club sang
and the principal made a few carefully studied im-
promptu remarks. Then he introduced Congressman
Kinney. It was at this moment, Gorman remembered,
that he really began to feel nervous. He did not know
what to do with his perspiring hands; he could not use
the sides of his new white flannels, yet the handkerchief
in his blue coat pocket, carefully arranged by his mother,
was untouchable. Each sentence which the Congressman
sent rolling from a full throat to the frescoed ceiling of
the auditorium brought Gorman a second closer to the

moment when he would have to stand up and walk forward. He had only three steps to go, but a man could stumble and fall flat in three steps.

"Sure, they tell us this isn't going to be a tough one but what I want to know is, if that's so, why the hell are they sending so much stuff along?"

"I never saw so many ships. Maybe they do expect something tough."

"That doesn't prove anything. Maybe they want to get it over in a hurry."

"Yeah, but maybe they know something they didn't tell us."

"Aw, nuts!"

And here, on this transport, Gorman relived that same feeling of that same moment when he waited. The speech had gone well; everybody said so.

And having identified the shadow of repetition, Gorman felt better and stretched out, completely relaxed. The morning would be just like the Commencement business. In that memory he had found for himself his own deep and personal reassurance.

Then he swung his feet over his bunk and kicked someone in the head.

"Hey, what the hell!"

"Where you going, out to a movie?"   .

Gorman said, "Going to take a leak."

"Use your helmet."

Gorman picked his way over outstretched bodies and lurched forward to a companionway, then went unsteadily into the long dark alley. He had a long way to go and felt his way along slowly.

Then he bumped into someone.

A woman's voice said, "Excuse me, do you know a sailor named Johnny Smith from South Dakota on board?"

"What? What?" Gorman was surprised to hear his own voice so high-pitched and strange. "No, ma'am, I don't know anyone by that name."

He turned as quick as he could and almost ran back to the hold. He found his way to his bunk again and leaned down to his friends. "Guess what I just bumped into," he whispered. "A dame!"

"What the hell you talking about?"

"Honest to God, a dame! And with the most wonderful voice I ever heard."

"Come on, Gorman, things ain't tough enough yet for you to go nuts."

"No, honest," Gorman insisted, "a dame, and she asked me if I knew a sailor named Johnny Smith."

"Good-looking?"

"Beautiful as hell," Gorman said, sure of it.

"Maybe it was a nurse."

Someone said, "Couldn't be. They all went on the hospital ships. I saw 'em embark this afternoon."

Someone else said, "It can't be a dame. Hell, we saw everyone embark and no dame came up the gangplank."

"Did you see the captain come aboard?" Gorman asked angrily.

"No, I didn't. What the hell's that got to do with it?"

"Because you didn't see him, does that mean he didn't come aboard?"

Someone said, "So there's a dame aboard. So what? One dame and nine hundred marines. Christ, what a ratio!"

"And with all the brass on board what chance has an ordinary leatherneck?"

Gorman was thinking to a deep conclusion. "You know what I think? I told you she had a wonderful voice, like the kind you hear in the movies at the end when the girl says to the boy, 'I love you too, Wallace.' I'll bet the girl aboard's a movie star."

"Now we know he's nuts."

Gorman went on with mounting excitement. "I'll bet there's a U.S.O. unit aboard." He thought of that for a moment with suspense and pleasure. Then came another conclusion. "And that fact ought to shut up you guys who're worrying about how tough it's going to be tomorrow."

Someone said grudgingly, "Maybe he's right, if he did meet a dame."

"Of course I'm right," Gorman insisted. "If we were going into anything tough they wouldn't be carrying a U.S.O. unit, would they?"

Someone said thoughtfully, "I hope to Christ it's not Joan Crawford. She reminds me too much of a girl who jilted me."

Gorman settled back easily and relaxed. "I don't give a damn who it is." He felt sure for the first time that he could really fall asleep. "For all I care, it could be Zasu Pitts."

A marine yawned loudly, then said, "Sure, any movie actress will do so long as she's a woman!"

*   *   *

The Captain was tired, far beyond the limit of his strength, tired to the point where even sleep did not help very much. A huge operation was over and the Task Force was back again at its base, after supporting yet one more invasion. Over the near-by waters its units lay as scattered and numerous as toys on a nursery floor.

This evening there had been a final summing-up on the flagship of the Force. Now the Captain rode back in a launch to his own ship, letting his shoulders droop and saying nothing. As always, while his ship was on a mission, he had not left the bridge. Now he had a chance to relax, but felt that he had lost the key that would unwind his nerves and let them loose again.

Beside him sat Lohrman, his executive officer. Because the Captain said nothing, no one spoke and there was no sound except for the quiet motor and the slip of the launch over quiet water. Not far ahead, under the stars and a shaving of moon, was the Captain's ship, the *Florida*.

Suddenly the Captain turned to Lohrman. "Commander Mitchell was certainly in good form tonight, wasn't he?"

"He had some good stories," Lohrman said. "I'll never forget the one he told about the New York girl who outdarwined Darwin and got silver fox skins from a wolf."

"I can hear you telling it for the next five years," the Captain said. "The story that interested me was the one he told about that girl, the girl they've reported seeing on so many different ships."

"Men under strain see funny things," Lohrman said. "Wanting a woman, then seeing her, doesn't ask too much of the imagination."

The Captain was not so sure. "I'm certain there's some ground for it. I've heard similar stories before. The sea always produces mysteries—miracles." He was silent again, but just for a moment. "I remember when I was an ensign on the *New York*, thirty-five years ago!" Something in the memory made him chuckle. "That's too long a story to tell now. One thing interested me in what Mitchell said. He told how everyone who saw the girl could agree on two things, her blond hair and her voice. I guess that's what sailors would like most—to see a woman's blond hair and to hear a low soft woman's voice. In fact," he said gently, almost wistfully, "it wouldn't be bad at all to see a good-looking woman, would it?"

"Any woman, Captain," Lohrman said gloomily.

The Captain laughed at that. "That's the one advantage the Army has over the Navy. They don't cut themselves off as we have to do."

The launch came to the ladder. The Captain hurried up the steps, returned the salute of the officer at the deck, and hurried off to his quarters.

He had a pleasant room, done in brown and green, as spacious and comfortable as any room on shore. His Filipino boy had put out his robe and pajamas. On the light oak desk, beneath a curtained porthole, was a pile of letters, magazines, and newspapers just in from the States. On a dresser near by were some family photographs showing a patrician gray-haired wife, a very beautiful daughter, and a young naval officer, his son.

Before opening his mail he took off his uniform and slipped into his robe. He took the first letter, from his wife, and settled back wearily in a broad green leather chair and let himself think of home, on a red clay shore

in eastern Maryland, of its trees, green lawns, and garden, and of the sheer and intimate pleasures every glimpse
of the low white house always implied.

His wife, as usual, had written little more than a note.
Washington was hot, servants were leaving, so and so
was home from overseas, so and so's son was reported lost,
the wife of Admiral Coring was not very well, some friends
from Annapolis had been down for the weekend. Not
very much in it, but she wrote almost every day and always had the gift of bringing home so near and so real
that for a moment the Captain could settle back and
imagine himself in the living room and catch the summer
breeze coming in from over the garden and the orchard.

In the same mood he slipped back to a thought that
came in recent weeks with increasing frequency. It was
not a happy thought nor one which he shared with anyone. It worried him to the point where, at times, he wondered if he knew his own mind.

For thirty-five years before 1942 he had alternated sea
duty with work in Washington, unfortunately, mostly the
latter. In those days the thought of a command, of one
continuous mission after another, had been so remote
that he had never let himself think of it. And now he had
had it, for two years. One mission after the other, with
time between only sufficient for refueling and restocking
ships, but insufficient for refueling and restocking a tired
man. He could imagine no greater reward now than to be
home again, without the responsibility for thousands of
men, a responsibility that grew heavier the longer it was
borne.

That consciousness of responsibility was something new
and troublesome. He wondered if other men noticed a
change in him, the change he was sure he knew in himself. If that change was permanent and serious then he
had no other honorable course but to ask for transfer to
shore duty.

He heard a sound at his door but did not look up. He
felt too tired even to raise his head. Usually the Filipino
boy came at this time for any last minute wishes. The

Captain called, "Nothing more tonight, José. Good night."

But the door opened and the Captain looked up, half startled.

A girl was there, asking, "Excuse me, but do you know a sailor named Johnny Smith from South Dakota on board?"

"I don't know," the Captain said, thoroughly friendly. "Won't you come in?"

Katie stood timidly by the door, ready to flee.

"I've heard about you, my dear," the Captain said. "Mitchell didn't describe you half well enough. Sit down, and tell me how you got here and what I can do."

Katie still hovered nervously near the door.

"Please stay for a moment. I've heard that you ask just one question, wait for an answer, then vanish."

Katie nodded.

"Tell me first how you come."

In a very few words Katie told him.

The Captain listened thoughtfully. "It must be nice to have such a charm. You wouldn't lend it for one night? There's a place in Maryland I'd like to see." Then he smiled. "Don't look so concerned. You see, my dear, my name is O'Reilly, and I believe in charms too. Any old sailor does. If it weren't for them and an occasional miracle, God alone knows how the Navy would operate."

Katie did not answer.

"What is the name of the sailor you want to find?"

"Johnny—Johnny Smith from South Dakota."

"Not an uncommon name," Captain O'Reilly said. "But perhaps I can help you find him. You don't know what ship he's on or what he does? Then tell me how you met him."

Still at the door, Katie told him, just as briefly as possible.

The Captain reached to his desk for pencil and paper. "That's not so hard, after all. What date did you meet him?"

"Last July seventh."

"Then all we have to do," O'Reilly said confidently, "is to find out what ship put into Brooklyn early that morning and left the same day. That will eliminate a lot of the Navy and narrow down our search. Then we can write the Bureau of Navy Personnel in Washington."

For the first time Katie smiled and a little of her timidity left her. "Would you really be kind enough to do all that?"

The Captain looked at her closely. "He'll be a very lucky sailor. But are you sure he wants to be found? A lot of sailors I've known went to sea purposely to avoid it."

"He will, if I just know where to write him," Katie said.

"Very well," O'Reilly answered gently, making a few notes. He asked Katie for her address, then said, "I promise to help, but I must ask a promise from you."

"Yes, sir."

"You must promise me you'll stop searching, my dear. You can rest quietly at night and not distract the Navy any further. Will you promise?"

After a moment's hesitation Katie nodded. "I'll promise."

"You've seen a lot of the Navy, haven't you?"

"Yes," Katie admitted.

"Few people have seen as much as you have—not even myself," O'Reilly continued. "If people ever ask you about it, tell them. Tell them it is a merciless and wretched world that forces men to have to be as brave as our sailors have to be. Maybe you and your Johnny can live in a more sensible world." He smiled. "And one that doesn't take you so awfully far from home."

He stood up from his chair. Before he could take a step toward her, she was gone. He followed her out into the companionway. A stiff strong breeze there quickly erased his last feeling of fatigue.

He returned to his cabin and sat looking at the data he had just written on his pad. Then he called for Lohrman, the executive officer.

"Sorry to disturb you at this time of night," O'Reilly

said, "but I wanted to see you. Remember that girl Mitchell spoke about? She has just been here visiting me."

Lohrman looked startled.

"I had quite a conversation with her," O'Reilly continued.

He reported it in detail, watching Lohrman's face from time to time.

Lohrman showed no reaction. When O'Reilly was finished, he said, "If you'll excuse me for saying so, you were awfully tired when I left you—you've been tired for the last few days."

O'Reilly agreed.

"The story of that girl was on your mind. You probably sat down, fell asleep—"

"And imagined it?" O'Reilly looked concerned. "That's what I decided a moment before I called you, as soon as I stepped out into the companionway and felt the strong fresh air."

"Sure," Lohrman said, suddenly very relieved. "That obviously is what it was."

"I'd agree, with relief," O'Reilly said, "but how did I happen to write a strange girl's name and address on this pad?"

Lohrman's face was always under control but his voice showed what he felt.

"Look, Captain, really—"

O'Reilly nodded. "If I've been seeing illusions then it's very obvious what my next step should be. I'm scarcely fit to command."

What Lohrman thought now showed on his face. "I'm sure you fell asleep."

"I don't know, frankly," O'Reilly said. "But I do know what to do. Suppose we send a message to Naval Intelligence in Washington and ask them to verify this girl's address. If she does live there and if there is such a person, then perhaps I've not turned senile." Then, equally firm, he said, "And if they find no such person, then I shall ask for retirement or shore duty at once."

Two days later O'Reilly, grinning from ear to ear,

showed Lohrman a message from Washington. It said,
"Katie Morrison lives at 183 York Street, Brooklyn."

*   *   *

Call them the meanest and most insignificant ships in
the Navy, the repair ships, but the men who sail them
won't mind what you call them so long as they can stay
on them. They never make the headlines or even the
communiqués. When one is bombed the dispatch tells of
"a light auxiliary vessel. . . ." They are nothing to look
at, squat, ugly, without speed, and with all the charm of
a seaborne garage. Yet no fleet wants to go anywhere without them.

Because they're supposed to stay away from the fighting they aren't even well armed. A few Bofors, a three-
inch gun fore and aft, maybe a couple of other pieces,
maybe not. Sailors assigned to them take one look and
squawk, "A hell of a lot of fighting we'll see on this floating toolshed."

But let no man question their importance. From cutting steel plate to fit torpedo holes, to master gear cutting,
dynamo winding, down to repairing the skipper's electric
razor, they work their miracles which, done day after day,
become routine.

But the repair ship *Corder* was not on routine as she
headed west, badly down at the port bow and making four
knots. She was in the condition of "Physician, heal thy-
self." A floating mine or perhaps a torpedo at dusk had
torn twenty feet from her port side. She lay on the water
like a breast-wounded duck, making for shore under diffi-
culties.

Her skipper ran a tight ship and shared generously
all praise received for routine miracles duly performed.
The result was crew morale so high that logging a man
was just about unheard of. From this happy family the
mine or torpedo took forty-nine men. Their loss was as
jagged a hole in the minds of the survivors as the gaping
toothy gap up at the bow. The loss went through the
whole crew complement.

"Tough to think of forty-nine men at once," the skipper told the first officer the next morning as he sat at his desk and glanced over the casualty roster. He looked up wearily. "All good men and hard to replace. It's tough enough to see one boy gone, let alone forty-nine." He turned from his desk. "Particularly Emonds." He had been the chief engineer. "We've been close friends for twenty years but never once the same ship together until we got this assignment three years ago. Sure, I hoped for something better than a repair ship—so did Emonds. But the fact that we were to be together at last somehow made a difference."

The skipper stood up. He looked tired. When he walked about his room his whole body showed his fatigue. "Tough on Emond's wife too," he said thoughtfully. "They live right across the street from my family in Boston. Four kids to put through school, all girls, and on a Navy pension." He picked up his pipe, put it in his mouth, then held the bowl with his hand as if it were a speaking tube. "That's what you always face in the Navy. That's what you're trained for, but you sort of forget it and you raise your families and then when it comes—!" He put his pipe down. "But, hell, when it comes, I guess death on land is as final as death at sea."

Down in the galley where Baker First Class Scully was gone, Robinson, his best friend said, "Why in the hell should it have gotten him? He has a mother and father who were crazy about him. Why didn't it get me? We were together all the time up to a minute before we got hit. Nobody in the world gives a damn about me, dead or alive, but I hate to think of Scully's old man. He runs a little German bakery up in Milwaukee and he was so proud of his kid. Every time he came home he had him baking pies and he'd put 'em in the window and advertise, 'Taste the pies our Navy eats!' "

Robinson shifted about uneasily. "It could just as well have been me. Somebody had to go forward to get some soap. I was about to go but I remembered some shirts I had soaking so Scully went instead. And here I am, thanks to a dirty shirt, and Scully's gone and his old man who was always blowing about his boy and the pies he could make—" Robinson scratched his head. "Who the hell decides when a guy's number's up, that's what I'd like to know?"

Up in the radio shack, Carlton, assistant chief operator, was talking to Sisson, the number three. The chief, Brewster, was gone. Carlton had in front of him a large manila envelope and a pile of papers covered with drawings, mostly crude, and many figures and computations.

"I can't make out a thing," Carlton said, pushing the papers aside. "Not a thing. And I doubt if anyone can."

"God knows, I can't," Sisson agreed.

"Hell of a note," Carlton said. "This is about all he leaves his wife and nobody can make head or tail of it."

Sisson glanced once more at the papers. "About four years steady work and all his time off—"

Carlton nodded, "And without a chance to finish it or to explain it to anyone who could understand."

Sisson said, "From the way he talked the last few weeks he seemed to think he had it." Then he frowned, "But he was awful secretive about it."

"Why the hell shouldn't he be?"

"I don't mean that—even if he'd explained I wouldn't have understood."

Carlton began to put the papers back in the envelope. "If his idea was any good," he said slowly, "he would have had a way to revolutionize radio, to upset the whole present structure. Something about the inherent radioactivity of all matter, but it was too deep for me. I just know that all the basic patents for radio tubes wouldn't have been worth a damn." He added proudly, "After all, Brewster was an M.I.T. graduate and he gave it all up, just to be a Navy radio operator."

"He'd have made a pile of dough."

Carlton nodded absently. Then he walked about, thinking his own thoughts. "That's the hell of war, the real hell—"

"I know what you're going to say," Sisson interrupted.

"I ought to—I've heard it a thousand times," he added defensively. "But there'll always be wars."

Carlton nodded slowly. "As long as there are men who want to fight them and men who think they can profit from them. But that's not what I was going to say. What I was going to say isn't new either, but it's awful goddam true—it's about those plans Brewster was working on, all junk now. Just think of all the plans and dreams and inventions and books and machines that were in men's minds as they went into war. Then a bullet or a bomb came along and all those wonderful dreams and ideas became worm food or fish food, and the world will never know what it has lost, only that it has lost."

Sisson nodded slowly, "Yeah, that's something to think about."

"But you don't like to think about it."

"No, I don't," Sisson admitted wearily. "There's nothing I can do about it." Then he asked briskly, "Shall I put Brewster's home address on this envelope and just mail it to his wife?"

In the machinist's quarters First Machinist's Mate Coogan was talking about his shipmate Mike Walthrop.

"Funny," he said gloomily, "when he was alive I felt he was the biggest rat in the world. Hell, he did do so many mean things to me, it makes me sore just to remember them. The last thing I said to him, just before he went forward and got his, was just what I felt. I told him, 'You wait till we get ashore, you rat. I'm going to beat the living muck right out of you.' And he knew that I meant it too."

The men gathered around looked up at Coogan, six-feet-four, and they knew he meant it too.

"Maybe some of the guys were picked up by other ships," someone said.

"Maybe," Coogan admitted. "There were other ships around. I hope to God they got Mike just so I can still get a crack at that jaw of his." He lit a cigarette and looked down at the end with no pleasure. "But what the hell, if he's gone, he's gone. You remember the last leave we had in Brooklyn, when we were in for just twelve hours?"

"Do we remember?" That came like a chorus.

"I had a girl there and I was goddam eager to see her. An awful easy lay but a hell of a good one. Mike knew her too—he ran into us once in a bar a year ago and I was a gentleman and introduced her to him. That was a mistake with Mike, ever being a gentleman when he was around. But I was, and the first thing he did was to ask for her address and phone number. But she wasn't any lady. She gave it to him right away without making him work for it.

"So, just before we went ashore the last time in Brooklyn he asked me to loan him twenty bucks. I gave it to him as we headed for the Sands Street gate. There he left me, running like hell, saying he had to catch a ferry to Bayonne where his brother lives. I had some breakfast and went around to the girl's house at a decent hour and damn if she wasn't gone, as early in the morning as that. And her neighbors said she'd gone out just a little while before with a sailor."

"Was it Mike?" someone asked.

Coogan nodded. "And on my twenty bucks! Well, I hung around town all day—even went to a movie. It was about sailors and the story was about a sailor who'd come ashore wanting to find a girl. On top of everything, imagine me running into a movie like that. So I came back to the ship and when Mike came aboard I accused him but he said, 'Hell, no, I was off seeing my niece in Bayonne, the one that looks like me.' If he had a niece that looked like him you could be damn sure he was the father!"

"He was good-looking though," someone said.

"Depends on taste," Coogan answered, "and on eyesight. Well, comes the first maildrop after that, and there's a letter from the dame in Brooklyn saying how sorry she was she didn't see me when the ship was in but Mike told her I was in the brig and wouldn't be let on shore."

Then Coogan put his cigarette out. "Well, what the hell—he's gone now. He never paid me back the twenty bucks, but what the hell, I even forgive him that. And the dame too. I'm glad he had fun with her, seeing it was the last chance he had, even if she was my girl."

At the stern a few of the deck crew sat listlessly, their backs resting against the shield of the stern gun. One stout sailor was doing the talking, what there was of it. Fourteen of the deck gang were gone. The torpedo had crashed right into their quarters and had taken others who were working up at the bow. "It'll take us a month to get back in shape," the sailor said gloomily.

"Even with replacements it won't seem like the same ship."

The sailor shook his head. "When you've been in the Navy as long as I have you get used to these things."

"Aw," one seaman argued, "you're not so tough, Lardlips."

"I'm plenty tough at times like this."

"You're going to miss a lot of those guys and you know it, so don't pretend."

"Sure, I'll miss 'em," Lardlips said with careful carelessness. "But sailors are sailors. They turn 'em out these days like a machine stamps out washers."

"What about Johnny Smith?" someone asked.

Lardlips' face quivered a little. "What about him?"

"You'll never find a guy to believe your yarns the way he did."

"Yeah," Lardlips agreed unwilling. "I guess I'll sort of miss him all right."

"Sure," someone said, "it was always 'Lardlips says—' with Johnny."

Lardlips nodded slowly, caught in a deep insoluble problem. "Maybe they picked the kid up." His face was gray. "Anyway, he was a good kid and no jerk. But that's the good thing about the Navy. There'll be other Johnnies coming along. They keep coming from their farms with the oats still in their hair and the only thing they ever had to do with water was to pump it into the cow barn. So we get 'em and make good sailors out of 'em. And Christ knows, they make good sailors."

3.

$\mathcal{A}$T LUSHMAN'S EIGHTY-TWO JOE, the tall, thin, pimply-faced counterman, usually boasted that he knew everything anyone could know about countergirls. He told that to Stella, the girl who came on at two each afternoon.

"I'm telling you," Joe said as he began to clean out the coffee urns, "I ought to know about 'em. I've worked with hundreds. I've seen 'em when they're putting in a whole day behind the counter even when they're worried sick about their baby at home with pneumonia, so that they hand a guy a glass of milk when he wants a dish of prunes and don't even look at him when he bawls them out for being stupid. I've seen 'em standing on the sides of their feet all day with their shoes off because they got various veins, but they go on working because they need the job so as to pay the rent while their husband's doing a stretch at Dannemora."

Stella nodded and grunted. She was heavy, blond, and experimenting with an upswept hairdo for the first time. As she cleaned the steam table, she was far more interested in wondering why no customers, not even the steady ones, commented on her hair.

"I could write a book about countergirls," Joe continued, "if anyone cared a damn about 'em, but I'm telling you, I can't figure Katie out. First, I don't know what the hell a good-looking girl like that goes on working here for when she's so unhappy, although she ain't as good-looking as she used to be. There's a funny kind of funny look on her face now. You ever seen her when a sailor comes up to the counter?"

"Nope." Stella was wondering whether the little hairs at the base of her neck were still caught in the upsweep or whether they stuck out like a hairy collar. She wished she could get to a mirror.

"Hey," Joe demanded, stopping his polishing for a moment. "You listening?"

"Yep."

"When a sailor comes up she just goes over his face with a fine comb, like—like she's looking for something hidden in it. You ever noticed that?"

"Nope." A black silk dress Stella saw on Atlantic Avenue for nine ninety-five would go well with the hairdo.

"Sometimes she seems like two people, sort of. One's her old self, the other's like someone far away, and more and more she's getting like that one. You noticed that?"

"Yep." Anyway, the hairdo showed her ears and she had pretty ears.

"I knew a guy like that once. Someone conked him on the head and he was like two other people the rest of his life. Maybe someone conked her. She said anything about something like that to you?"

"Nope."

"I saw something like that in the movies too once, with Boris Karloff. You like Boris Karloff?"

"Nope." With a little practice she could do her hair herself as well as the hairdresser.

"You know something funny? I was reading a racing form yesterday and there was a horse named Dr. Jekyll in the fifth race. That made me think of Katie, so I put two bucks on the nose. You know what?"

"Nope."

"The horse lost." Joe put one last swipe on the urn, then closed the box of polish.

*   *   *

Up on Broadway at Porkel's picture gallery Porkel was standing near the door looking at a photograph. His partner Hosenfenster came in from lunch wearing a new checked overcoat with modish muskrat collar.

"Hey, Hosie," Porkel said, holding out the picture to him. "Remember these people?"

Hosie looked at the picture of a tall thin sailor with his arm on the shoulder of a less tall but well-built girl, taken against a backdrop of Manhattan. "It's a copy of one of our jobs," Hosie said. "That's all I know."

"You don't remember them at all?"

"My God, no! If I remembered all our customers I'd have nightmares in daytime. What about them—the cops after them?"

"The girl was in here and gave me this copy," Porkel explained. "I remember her, her eyes, that is. She and the sailor were in early one morning last summer."

"Yeah?" Hosie yawned.

"Now she comes in, pathetic like. Something awfully funny about her. She wants to find the sailor and she left the picture and her address in case he ever comes in again."

"There's millions of girls hunting for sailors," Hosie said, taking off the coat and carefully smoothing the collar. "The whole country's full of girls each hunting for some one sailor. And if ever they find them the Navy'll have a tougher time than they ever had in the Pacific."

Porkel shook his head. "This girl's different. I had the funniest feeling that even when she talked to me she wasn't quite here and that she was hunting for a guy who wasn't there either. Like a ghost hunting a ghost."

"You've been drinking too much coffee," Hosie said, hanging his coat up in a closet over hooks filled with wedding dresses. "We ought to close nights in winter, Porkel. We don't make enough to pay for the lights, let alone the coffee you have to drink. Not actually."

*   *   *

In the lobby of the Waldorf Mrs. O'Geoghan was finishing mopping the floor near the main entrance. She put the mop through the wringer with more energy than the job needed and almost upset the bucket over the floor.

Mrs. Dolan, a thin-faced woman who was dusting the

furniture, looked over to Mrs. O'Geoghan. "You're not yourself this morning."

"And who would I be if not meself?" Mrs. O'Geoghan demanded.

Mrs. Dolan was not prepared to answer that.

"In truth, I'm not meself," Mrs. O'Geoghan admitted, going over the floor again with dry mop. "You remember Katie Morrison I was telling you about who worked here not two years ago? I saw her last night and I can't get her face out of my mind."

Mrs. Dolan sympathized with that. "When that happens it's like having your brain sprout eyes, nose, ears, and mouth that never stop tickling you."

"I worry about her," Mrs. O'Geoghan confessed. "I worry about her more than my five sons off to the Pacific wars. To me she's like my next and nighest."

"A daughter can worry you that way," Mrs. Dolan agreed, shaking out her dustcloth. "After all, men are supposed to get into trouble and they're used to sniveling out. But when a girl's in trouble it's like having a rocky hill grow on your shoulders."

"And this isn't ordinary trouble where you could stand by until the baby is born. Nothing like that." Mrs. O'Geoghan shook her head. "This is rare and frightful trouble." She lowered her voice although no one else was near by. "She's in love with a dead man."

"Merciful Mary in Heaven!" Mrs. Dolan looked as frightened as she sounded.

Mrs. O'Geoghan explained further, "Or, more proper, with a man she won't believe dead. He was submarined and one officer wrote her he is presumably lost. That's what he wrote, the very words. His name was O'Reilly and anyone named O'Reilly ought to have better sense than to leave such ground for lingering doubt in her mind. So Katie takes that to mean he's alive somewhere perhaps and she won't listen to anything else although I tramp to the edge of my mind trying to find some way to bring her back to her proper senses."

"Death's harder when you're young," Mrs. Dolan said.

"Yet, in a way, it's easier too. You have life ahead when you're young, but when you're old you know ahead of you is only loneliness to the end."

Mrs. O'Geoghan nodded absently. "And Katie goes on searching though I tell her she should leave her old ways and even New York and go away somewhere and forget. Then the trouble might end for her." She shook her head hopelessly. "You wouldn't know her now, so thin and her face the color and shape of Michael Foran's ghost that used to come down of nights from the hills behind Galway." She shook her head more vigorously to dislodge the memory. "I tell you, Mrs. Dolan, there's no look on the human face like that of one always searching and searching with never the littlest hope of ever finding."

Mrs. Dolan agreed, then went back to her work, saying nothing more until everything was finished. Without a word Mrs. O'Geoghan came to her, with pail and mop swinging in her hand, and she and Mrs. Dolan started from the lobby to their lockers below, their workday done.

"I've been thinking about Katie," Mrs. O'Geoghan said thoughtfully, "and the pain in her and the wanting that will never end, and then about all the other women in the world like her. There's no street in the world today, in winter or summer, Mrs. Dolan, where women don't walk their way in grief. In a manner of speaking, all those women all over the world are sisters today. It's a pitiful thing. It makes you think, Mrs. Dolan."

*   *   *

Summer or winter the men back from the sea pass along the dingy length of Sands Street. In winter the street is changed. The clothing stores display mostly blue uniforms and the unsold jewelry on the window shelves shows an added edge of tarnish. The tattoo designs, framed and displayed in the "studios," are more sunfaded. The Filipino restaurants no longer prop chairs outside their windows for passing friends from among the ships' stewards. The wind from the harbor blows knife-sharp but is never able to scrape the street clean of its grime and odor. The odors are still heavy, bilge-musty, and damp, but now they carry the edged pungence of coal smoke. The early morning fog comes in thicker and drapes the dusty buildings like soiled and streaked cotton. On winter mornings it hangs late over the street.

Some of the sailors who came along the winter street in early morning saw a girl come out of the mist, as sudden as unexpected landfall. A cloth coat was wrapped tightly around her slim body. She moved fast and sure, and the sailor was the more surprised when she suddenly stopped in front of him, almost blocking his way. Without seeing clearly in the morning gray each sailor was sure the girl's eyes were cutting through the mist to search his face. Then each heard the same question asked in a strange flat voice, "Do you know Johny Smith, a sailor from South Dakota?"

Usually they answered, "No," and before they could say anything else the girl was gone. The echo of her tapping heels went quickly in the distance. In a moment she was out of sound and sight, leaving each sailor questioning his own sight and hearing, sometimes his sanity, and usually his sobriety.

At times it was not quite like that. On one black morning Chief Yeoman Martin, thirty-five years in the Navy, came from the Yard, eager to get to his wife and four kids in Seaside Park. It was icy cold and a whipsnap of snow flicked the morning darkness. He saw dimly the figure of a girl coming a short way off up the street, walking quickly and alone, and he wondered why any girl would be out at that time of the morning.

Katie's question to him so surprised him that he fumbled with the cigarette in his hand and dropped it.

"I know a Johnny Smith on my ship," Martin said thoughtfully, "but I don't .think he comes from South Dakota." He felt uneasy and wanted to hurry on, yet something in Katie's voice held him.

"And is he young and dark-haired?"

"Smittie? Forty and bald as the forward deck."

In a lifeless voice Katie said, "My Johnny Smith may not be alive but I have to know. I have to know!"

Martin put his hand to his face as against a sudden burst of cold air, but as much to restrain a thought that crossed his mind.

"They said my Johnny was presumed lost," Katie continued.

The girl had to be human; only a human voice could carry such pain, and that satisfied Martin's sudden thought.

"If they say that, miss," he said gently, "he's probably gone. They're awful careful in those reports. It's a shame but—"

Katie cut him off. "But couldn't he possibly be alive somewhere?"

"There's always that chance," Martin admitted, "but it's so slim."

Then Katie turned and hurried away. The wind rose colder with the sound of a sob and with sharper bite. Martin was suddenly conscious of an even deeper desire for light and warmth and for the surety of his home, wife, and his children, and he almost raced up the street.

On another dark morning a tall young sailor came along the street, his hands in the side pockets of his short jacket, swinging as he walked. He whistled to himself as he saw Katie approaching a few feet away. He had his own question ready as he came near but Katie's question caught him unawares.

"Johnny Smith, from South Dakota?" he repeated cheerfully after a moment's hesitation. "Sure, I know him well. He's one of my best friends. Salt of the earth, Johnny."

Katie lifted her head and stared at him and asked slowly, "And is he well?" An uncontrollable tremor streaked her voice.

"Sure, fine, but he can't get ashore for a couple of days."

With voice still tremulous Katie said, "He was presumed lost."

"That was nothing," the sailor said, scoffing. "Just a ducking—happens all the time in the Navy."

Katie had other questions but at the moment what the sailor said choked the words in her throat.

"Say, baby, what's your name?"

"Katie." Her voice was low and deep as of old.

"Now that's a coincidence," the sailor answered heartily. "Johnny told me he had a good friend Katie here in town. He was going to give me your address but I got away from the ship too soon."

Katie bit her lip. Her voice filled with tears. "He never knew my address. You're cruel, cruel, cruel!" Then she turned and ran. The sailor reached out for her but she was gone.

He shrugged his shoulders and went on up the street. But when he got back to his ship he had a story to tell and he told it again and again, always saying, "Honest to God, the dame was like a ghost!"

So Katie lived each morning and in each hour of the day in her own gray world where the only light from far beyond was hope. She lived driven by some compulsion and she knew it. "They who search to no avail," Mrs. O'Geoghan had said, "might never quite return to themselves again." Nor would Katie have had it otherwise.

She went on in unbroken grayness, feeling as she had felt when she moved among the ships, something of a shadow apart from herself. At the sight of every tall lithe sailor her heart began to race; after each disappointment the pain of disillusion was a little sharper. And the small hope that was left shriveled the more with each passing day, and no man nor miracle nor magic could help.

And there the forlorn story might have ended, and no one could have changed it a whit. To the many stories told on shipboard of the girl who appeared suddenly, in whose eyes was living flame, might have been added stories told of a girl seen in the dawn on Sands Street.

*   *   *

There came one wet and dripping morning hung with

thick fog. The harbor wind tried to clear it but could only move great stringy bursts of it along the street as the July wind moves the white clouds of summer.

That morning Katie woke, sure she had overslept. She dressed quickly, wrapped her cloth coat tightly around her, then hurried down the creaking stairs and into the empty street. The fog fitted close as gray linen and at times was so thick she could not see a hand held trembling near her searching eyes. To the clicking echo of her own heels she walked rapidly over the rutted sidewalks of Gold Street and turned into Sands Street.

Somewhere, far ahead, were the muffled steps of a few hurrying men.

She came near the place where she and Johnny had first met. Whenever she passed it, hope and the memory set her trembling. Time and again, from a short way off, she saw the figure of a man waiting here; when she spoke to him no answer came back, and she was left to stare through illusion at nothingness.

This morning the street was so foggy that even the meeting place did not show clear, but she turned to it as she passed, the throb of her pulse a steady beat in her forehead. Dimly through the mist she saw, as so frequently, a figure slouched against the building. She was certain it was a sailor and certain too that he was only imagination, as tantalizing as always, as always ready to vanish should she put out a hand to him.

But, as always, she stopped to ask, "Excuse me, but do you know Johnny Smith, a sailor from South Dakota?"

When no answer came immediately she blinked, whisked her hand across her eyes, and turned to hurry on.

The sound of a sigh in the mist made her stop. Behind her a voice, as lifeless and weary as her own, said, "Johnny Smith, a sailor from South Dakota?"

For a second Katie stood still, shivering at illusion too real to be sanity. She knew that voice, no matter what pain or hurt might mask it, and she ran back, her arms wide, crying, "Johnny, Johnny, Johnny!"

Everything in her reached out to him, and as she

touched him and found him real she knew this was no illusion.

"Oh, Johnny! Johnny Smith!"

She stumbled into his arms but he was as unresponsive as a telephone pole.

Gently but impersonally he said, "How do you know my name?"

"Johnny!" Katie's voice crackled with laughter, with the joy of a long search over. "Johnny, I'm Katie."

His arms fell awkwardly to his side. "I don't remember any Katie."

"Katie, who was with you here in Brooklyn, right on this same street, at this same place."

"I don't remember," he repeated dully.

For a second, in turbulent happiness mixed with bewilderment, Katie wondered if she were playing one last horrible trick on herself. She put her hands up to his shoulders. They were solid and broad. She looked up at him. He was tall, slim, the hair beneath his cap seemed dark, and his face, framed by his jacket collar, was the face of the Johnny she had known.

"It was that way when they picked me up." His voice was flat and monotonous. "I don't remember anything except what people told me at the hospital."

"You will, you will, Johnny." Katie was certain now that he was real and she real beside him.

"They said my fingerprints showed I was Johnny Smith."

"Of course you are."

"You called me by that name but are you sure?"

"Sure?" Katie even laughed. "I'd have known you anywhere. Didn't I recognize your voice in the fog? Oh, Johnny, I searched all over for you."

"How well did you know me?"

"Very well, Johnny."

"And for how long? When?"

"Last summer. Not for long but I've never forgotten a minute of it."

"Maybe you've got me mixed up with someone else

like me," Johnny insisted. "Maybe they made a mistake in the fingerprint records and I'm really someone else, because I can't remember anything about Johnny Smith."

She stepped back, confused, feeling the deep throb within her stop in mid-beat.

"I only know what people tell me, and how can I be sure they're right?" The pain in his voice and the helplessness were as real as a choking hand across his windpipe. "And nothing will ever be right until I can remember for myself."

"Oh, Johnny, I can help you remember." Katie realized with a sudden sense of power that he needed her. "I'm sure I can."

"I don't know." He seemed all lost. "I just don't know."

The fog came suddenly thicker down the street. Johnny sounded buried in it, and Katie knew well that feeling.

But she felt him hold tightly to her arm, grateful for any little support, as he asked, "If you really knew me, have I changed? Why don't I remember you?"

"Don't you remember a girl named Katie at all?"

He shook his head. "I don't remember any dames."

Not far off were the dim lights of the Coffee Pot where they had first gone on that July morning. Katie said gently, "Walk with me to the light. Maybe if you see me in the light you'll remember."

Like an obedient little boy who did not want to let go, he came with her. When they reached the fog-ringed light he swung her around and searched her face. On his face she could see no sign of recognition.

She suggested quietly, "Let's go inside for coffee. I'm cold." Leading the way into the place, she hoped that the former attendant might still be here, as another aid to memory. He was gone. An elderly man, thin, gaunt, and bony, was in his place.

After ordering coffee, Katie waited for Johnny to speak. He stared at her, blinking in the bright light, then shook his head. "I'm sure I never saw hair or eyes like yours before. I don't believe I'd forget hair and eyes like yours."

"That's what you said the first time we met."

"How do I know there ever was a first time?"

Katie quickly opened her handbag and brought out a photograph. "We had this taken when we were together."

"A picture—of me?" Johnny studied the print for a long time, ignoring the coffee put in front of him. The strain bitten deep in his face was not new to Katie; she had seen lines like those on her own. When he examined the picture she watched him closely. He was thinner, much older, his boyishness gone. The wrinkles on his forehead were little ragged waves. Looking at the picture, he had gone deep into his mind, and Katie waited with body tight for what he might find there.

At last he put the picture down. "This could be me," he admitted. "But couldn't it just as well be someone who looked like me?"

"Oh, Johnny!" Katie knew in a cold flash that he was as far away as ever, with a great barrier still between them for her to break through and with no clear idea of the way. And she felt dropped from a great height.

"I don't even remember having the picture taken," he added. "That's what I was trying to remember too. You wouldn't think a guy'd forget that." He shook his head. "There's just one thing I remembered all by myself, that no one told me. I remembered that once I came here on this street near the Navy Yard early in the morning and something happened."

"What was it?"

"I got hospital permission to come early this morning to see if I could remember. But I can't. I don't know if it was good or bad or what."

That might offer a way to him and Katie took it eagerly. "We met right here, Johnny. Maybe that's what it was you remembered. Then we went to Manhattan and spent a morning together."

"Just a morning?"

Katie nodded. "And we went around doing things you wanted to do." She paused, ready to tell the whole story.

Johnny snapped, "Why just a morning?"

"We separated suddenly, that's all."

Johnny shook his head. To his own uncertainty was added suspicion. "As sudden as that? That just doesn't make sense. And you never saw me or heard from me again?"

Katie started to explain. "No, but—"

"That makes the Johnny Smith you knew one fine heel if you ask me. Christ, what a guy! That is, if what you say is true."

His sudden doubt stopped Katie short. This was the same sort of lack of trust he had shown on that July morning. She thought desperately and tried something else. "Don't you remember Lardlips who was on your ship?"

He shook his head. "They've named all kinds of names to me at the hospital but they're just names. That would be easiest of all, to go to my ship, but they say she's in the Pacific." His shoulders drooped and even deeper worry marked his face. "I have to remember things for myself."

"I could help perhaps, Johnny," Katie said quietly, "if you'd just believe me."

"Believing's got nothing to do with it." His voice flared loud for a second. "It's just that I want to be—well, I want to know it all by myself. I got to."

Katie felt beaten. They drank their coffee in silence. The only noise in the room was that of rattling dishes as the attendant rearranged the pastry display in the glass case.

Johnny put down his cup and rustled about in his chair. "A doctor at the hospital said something funny," he admitted slowly. "He said maybe I was uncertain and scared to pick up any one identity because I really wanted it that way. He said maybe I was afraid to come back to the world, what he calls the real world. That's what he said and when he talked to me he sounded awful baffled." Johnny's mouth drooped at the corners and his restlessness mounted. "But it doesn't help a damn to know that." He glanced up at the clock on the wall and compared the time on his wristwatch.

Katie felt emptied of words or feeling. She had found Johnny but only a little of him. Now he showed every sign of wanting to run.

He lit a cigarette while his gaze moved jerkily around the room, from the clock to the door to the counterman, back to the clock, then to the street outside. With some funny pride he said, "The doctor said I was quite a case. And he said maybe it will take a miracle to bring me back."

In answer Katie again fished inside her handbag, where she always had the coin. Perhaps the sight of it might remind him of his stay in Belfast, might let him recall something by himself. The miracle he wanted might not be far away. Without a word she handed the coin to him.

He took it almost unwillingly, asking, "What's that?"

"You gave me a present of it on that morning."

Johnny turned the coin in his hand and examined both sides. He shook his head in disappointment. "Not much of a present."

Katie continued, "You said you got it in Belfast. Do you remember ever being in Belfast?"

· After a moment of intense thought he said, "No, I don't remember anywhere I ever was."

Smiling to herself Katie said very casually, "I wish you'd get everything you want, Johnny."

She awaited his answer, watching his face, his eyes, his lips, knowing her own breath came suddenly faster. He was still looking at the coin as he asked, "What did you say?"

"I said, I wish you'd get everything you want." For Katie each split second was long-drawn and nerve-tearing.

He shook his head. "First I got to know what that is." He handed back the coin. "I don't remember this at all."

With the coin held tight in her hand Katie said, "I wish you'd find the real Johnny Smith for yourself, by yourself."

Johnny shook his head. "I have to find out more about him first. And I don't like what I heard about him from you."

She pressed the coin in her hand until she could feel its edges in her palm and the coin itself hot and moist. Once again, almost desperately, she tried to force him to join her in any wish. "I wish you'd get back all the memories you want."

He did not answer that.

"Don't you?" Katie insisted, her voice as tight as her clenched fist.

"Don't I what?"

"Don't you wish you'd get your memory back, right now?"

"The doctor says," Johnny answered mechanically, "that maybe deep down inside of me something holds me back."

Feeling exasperated, foolish, and helpless all at the same time, Katie asked, "Don't you wish for anything?"

"What good does wishing do?" Johnny was annoyed. "I've tried that. Are we playing some kids' game?"

"No," Katie said seriously, "but don't you really wish for something?"

He nodded. "Sometimes I do."

"What is it?" Katie held her breath.

"Sometimes I wish I were back on my ship, whatever it was. I hear sailors always feel sort of safe on their ship."

Katie sat with her mouth caught open. "And for nothing else?"

He looked up at the clock on the wall. "And sometimes when I get tired I wish the hospital wouldn't let me out."

Katie dropped the coin back in her handbag. She knew her face was red, her throat trembling and tightening. She answered sharply, "And you probably wish that people would let you alone too, and not try to help?"

"Sometimes I do," Johnny admitted.

From that sentence she understood more than from anything else he had said. She pushed her chair back. Its legs screeched on the tile floor. "You don't need any miracle to bring you back, Johnny. You just have to want to, to want to come back, that's all. You like it this way because

you're afraid of being a real man and taking what comes."
She stood up, not stopped by the sudden helplessness on
his face. "I'm going to leave you because what you've got
to do you've got to do by yourself." She drew her coat
around her. "You can go back to the hospital or to your
ship. You're just as stubborn as when I knew you, as stubborn and afraid too."

As if he were pleased to hear anything about himself
so long as it was specific, Johnny asked, "Was I really
stubborn and afraid?"

"Just the same," Katie said. "You haven't changed."
Anger if nothing else, had moved him a little. She glanced
at the counterman. He was listening, with both bony el-
bows propped on the counter, but Katie ignored him. She
turned again on Johnny. "I'm the only person around
who knows anything about you, about South Dakota
and Lardlips and ducks—" She felt she was about to cry
but she choked it back in her throat. "I could help if you
weren't scared, but I'm going to walk right out and leave
you now." She pulled the belt of her coat tight. "I met
you and I fell in love with you and then we separated and
now we'll be separating again but this time because I want
it that way. And you can go alone and I'll go alone never
knowing what we might have found together."

Without any other word she started for the door. The
counterman stood up and stared at what he was seeing.

At the door Katie heard behind her the noise of a scrap-
ing chair but she did not turn. In a few quick steps Johnny was beside her.

"Katie!" He took her arm. "Honest, I don't want to
be alone."

Katie swung around to him, her face still flaming.
"Why not? You might even be happy that way." She
added, "Most of what you have to do for yourself, you
have to do alone anyway."

"All right, but I don't want to be alone when I'm doing it."

Katie was not ready to accept that so rapidly. "Tell me
that you really want to find yourself. Tell me, right now."

"Of course I do, Katie."

"Tell me you won't be afraid of anything you find."

He hesitated for a moment. His glance met her steady gaze, dropped, then returned. "I won't be afraid of anything." He put his hand on her arm. "You said we started out from here once for a morning in New York. Maybe we could start out like that now, together, and maybe we might find lots of things to remember."

Katie smiled broadly, her eyes alight, and took his hand. "I already have memories enough for the two of us."

The door closed behind them and they were gone arm in arm into the low white fog that rose from the river and the sea.

THE END